BUILD
UNIVERSES

Roma il 16 aprile 2023

With a ton of

love and

laughs

Anne Lamunière
and
Maria Antonietta Bonacci Potsios

A SIMPLE STORY
ME, MYSELF AND HER

© 2022 **Europe Books** | London
www.europebooks.co.uk – info@europebooks.co.uk

ISBN 979-12-201-2440-9
First edition: August 2022

A SIMPLE STORY
ME, MYSELF AND HER

To Amina.
To Balthazar, Charly, Francesco, Giorgio, Julien,
Stefano.
And to all those who inspired us and are in our hearts.

Il y a des jours, des mois, des années interminables
où il ne se passe presque rien.
Il y a des minutes et des secondes qui contiennent tout un
monde.

There are days, months, endless years when nothing happens.
There are minutes and seconds that contain an entire world.

Jean d'Ormesson

AUTHORS' NOTE

So here you are, opening the first page of this Simple Story.

Before you continue, you must be aware that this book does not have the pretension of being a literary masterpiece, nor was it ever meant to be. It is the story of a woman, a child, a family, and a terrible illness. Love, hate, friendship, loss, laughter, and tears.

When COVID-19 emerged and obliged us to confine in our homes and confront ourselves with our past lives and present issues, we started an email exchange based on a quote by Jean d'Ormesson:

There are days, months, endless years when nothing happens. There are minutes and seconds that contain an entire world.

It seemed to us that this quote represented what we were going through: our lives had and were going to change for a lapse of time. Day after day, we wrote in turns, correcting and adding to each other's text. A paragraph to a page at a time ended up being our common story. Neither knew what the other was going to write until the next day. Just like in life: one never knows what is going to happen. One adapts to what comes along, whether good or bad.

Based on true facts, true feelings, and past memories, this short story is fictional. Some of you will recognize themselves and some will feel like they are missing. Truthfully, the characters and adventures are a cocktail of the people we have known and the stories we have lived.

At the end of the first confinement in May 2020, these were the pages that had been written. With great wisdom and skill, the writer Elie Kerrigan helped edit it into the version you will read. The artist Florence Schlegel embellished it with her superb drawings. We thank them both from the bottom of our hearts.

Anne & Maria Antonietta

PART I

NEW YORK CITY – 2004

When she woke up, Mia felt strange. She had woken up several times in the middle of the night due to disturbing dreams: tigers climbing up the balcony and horses swimming in the sea. Sweaty and cold, she wondered for a split second what the matter was, but was too tired and chose instead to close her eyes again.

Was there anything in her life worth living for? I often heard her ask herself that question.

It was the water she loved and, almost obsessively, needed most. Water! The sea, swimming pools, rivers, and lakes: they had the power to cleanse by first pulling one onto the shore and then lapping you in a manner as to reabsorb all that was foul, as if it had never been there in the first place. She dreamt of us on the beach, sometimes walking hand in hand with friends, at others sunbathing, with my auburn hair sweeping her tears away.

It was night-time. I could not tell exactly the hour because I was too small to read a watch, but I knew it was dark. My little bed was next to hers and I felt that she was worried and wished for morning to stretch its open arms to embrace us with cheerful news.

The previous evening she'd finally been able to laugh with her nurse friend; they had played with me and laughed so hard that tears had filled their eyes. Once they made sure I was sleeping (I was pretending), they'd gone out for drinks and I was finally able to fall asleep with the thought of her being happy. I could not tell why, but I always sensed her fear; I could sense it in her eyes, in her smile, in her face. At times, I wished she could've relaxed, at least, once in a while.

As far as I was concerned, I was doing well, apart from the beeping sound that I so often heard and which, at night, really got on my nerves, but for the most part, I was okay. I could not complain of a lack of love or attention for it was rather the opposite. However, it was early morning now and I wondered how much longer we'd be staying in this place.

The breathing in her sleep kept me going. I loved to hear the smooth snoring of her calm body. For a while, everything was fine, peaceful, and pleasant. We were together, breathing next to each other.

Beep, beep, beep, beep...

Suddenly, amid this wonderful moment in time, I felt a deep pain in my body... What? *Boom: Black, light, black, light.... Beep, beep, black, light...* I hear her shouting, she's awake, she's calling my name and I'm unable to answer her back... *black, light, beep, black, black, light...*

Beeeeeeeeeeeeeeeeeeeeppp.

The pain begins to ease and slowly disappears... my body feels free and light; I'm floating into a bright pink sunshine.

I see her. She'll survive. I'm off to a new dance.

We had parted. As fast as I rose up into the sky, she descended at the same speed into the darkness of her soul, until she arrived in that special place where she was profoundly alone.

As for myself, I was simply relieved that the *beeping* had finally stopped.

NEW YORK – 2005, The day before the Vernissage

Mia always had difficulty getting ready on time in the morning. She always woke up tired, probably more so than when she had gone to bed.

Once she had managed to drink a cup of coffee and a nasty-looking orange vitamin drink, she would put on a dress. Her biggest challenge was finding a pair of pantyhose with no holes – this routine drove her nuts every single morning. She knew she had to play-act and quickly gravitate towards a new life with Marco who was already ten years old. Besides, work was scarce these days...

As she rushed out of the door, something got caught on her heel. "Shit!" It was a tie lying on the floor! What the hell was it doing there? I am not sure she really remembered much about the tie – in any case, she had no time for it now. She had to run to her meeting.

She was late and jumped into a cab. Always in a rush! Then again, I guess that was why she loved New York: everyone was always on the move, regardless of the time of day or night.

These were strange and trying times for Mia: looking at New York out the taxi window, immured within her "new self", with the memory of me still fresh in her soul, she struggled to be the person I would be proud of, that I would look up to.

And I do.

From above, looking down, with a mixture of sorrow and compassion, hoping that she wins this struggle with herself and comes out on top.

New York is not for chickens. There are millions of anonymous people, talented, ambitious, doing whatever it takes, twenty-four-seven, to make sure their dreams come true. All this creativity in one single place under the sun… No wonder she decided to stay in this sprawling metropolis. It either makes or breaks you but leaves no one indifferent; New York is a restless *tourbillon* of energy which constantly opens doors to new adventures. So much creativity! This is why she had decided to stay: she could sculpt *things* out of clay, glass, wood, metal; shape and color her feelings, and infuse life and meaning into concepts that only recently were made clear and could be appreciated and understood.

Feeling rather nauseous after the Pakistani taxi driver had blasted the music and kept hitting the breaks every two seconds, she finally reached her destination: a storage building somewhere in the Meat Packing District. As she stepped out of the taxi, her pantyhose ripped, "Fuck!" she swore, again. She always swears… Sometimes I wish she would just calm down. If she could only see what I see.

Louis, who was smoking one of his Vogue cigarettes on the sidewalk, overheard her and broke into a laugh. Was she lucky to have him? Time would tell; for now, he was her gallerist, her friend, and her precious support. The show she had been working on included more than twenty pieces, all devoted to the theme of destruction.

He stopped laughing and gave her a big hug:

"Don't worry darling, ripped pantyhose are so Vivienne Westwood!"

"*Merde,* Louis!" she said, as she collapsed into his arms.

Louis is French and regarded as a very fashionable fellow. I still recall the three-piece baby dress he gave me when I was born. Mia and Dad had me wear it on special occasions.

Mia's *vernissage* was the following day, and naturally, she was anxious. Louis had convinced her that her *things* were actually good sculptures. Now, twenty-four hours before D-day and with more than one hundred guests confirmed, she was having second thoughts – wondering why the hell she was going through with this. Deep down she knew she really needed the money, and this might turn out to be the break that she needed so badly. The only certainty at this precise moment was that she needed a strong drink to steady her nerves and help her get through this meeting.

Seeing her now, all worked up inside the gallery, pacing about, brought back memories of more peaceful and calmer times – times when we used to climb on the J Train over the Williamsburg Bridge, then the 6 to end up in Central Park. They would take pictures of me and film me as I wobbled along. Marco and Dad were there, too, and of course, Jules, our *Dachshund,* following faithfully behind.

Those were happy moments frozen in time by way of photographs and camcorder memories. A time of blissful innocence, before the demons of disruption dragged our little family into the maws of malicious mayhem. As soon as all details for the following day's big event had been settled, Mia said goodbye and headed home.

On opening the door to her apartment, she was confronted with the exact same mess she had left behind several hours earlier. She kicked off her high heels, then dropped her bag, followed by her coat, and headed to the fridge to grab an open bottle of rosé. She filled her mouth with a glass of *Bandol* and went over to the phone to call Marco.

"*Ciao,* it's me. *Come va?*"

19

"Fine thanks. Let me go get Marco for you."

The conversation between her and Dad had been reduced to the bare minimum ever since my departure, and I could tell it was not getting any better with time.

"Mommy, *ciao!*"

"*Amore, ciao,* how are you? How was school today?"

"Fine, we did lots of drawings and the alphabet."

"Good! Did you do a drawing for me?"

"Yes."

"Do you have it or did you leave it at school?"

"I have it and it's filled with blue like the color of your eyes. I also did a drawing for Angela. Do you think she will see it from where she is?"

"That's wonderful! I am sure, no matter where she is, she'll love it. No doubt."

Of course, I could see it. They hung up blowing imaginary kisses to each other. Mia turned towards the window to watch the setting sun in the distance, beyond the Brooklyn water towers, as it slowly covered the buildings with a mantle of gold, purple and lead-like blue streaks of dying light. It was a moving picture and had become a sort of ritual for her. She associated this natural display of color with me. As if it were a sign solely for her eyes, letting her know that even if we had parted, we were still very much together, bound by an everlasting communion of love. And through her tears, she kept a steady gaze until all the positive energy once again steadied her breathing and she was once more at peace with herself and the world.

After downing a few more glasses of wine and biting directly into a chunk of *Gruyere*, she decided it was time to put some order to the mess all around her. She started, almost maniacally, dusting and ordering.

The Witches had promised to be in town for her opening, and she figured that it might as well be in a reasonable state before it was trashed again. A clean and tidy place was a reflection of a clear and uncluttered mind. Or so she hoped. The pile of plates and glasses in the sink (traces of the previous night's carousing) were finally washed and the tie was picked up from the floor and put away.

The tie... from what I could tell, belonged to someone called Hermès.

I personally do not feel entitled to comment on this or any other tie, except to say that I guess ties are like teddy bears: you hold on to them at night for protective reasons when scared, and later toss them any old place in the morning when you wake up. Sooner or later, you are desperately looking for them again.

ST. GALLEN – 1986, The Rosenberg

With hands pressed against her belly, feeling as if her guts were about to explode, thirteen-year-old Mia sat at her new desk, struggling to hold back her tears.

Beyond the classroom's window, she watched the rain lashing down on the ugly-looking pine trees. The classroom was headed by a weird-looking biology teacher who wore horrible leather sandals which made her want to puke. All around her sat a bunch of strangers; some looking just as unhappy as her whilst others were already grinning, passing notes to one another.

'Fucking idiots...' Mia thought.

She had no intention of listening to that repulsive individual sitting at his desk, playing Jesus with his disgusting yellow toes sticking out. There was no way she was going to stay in this "prison": a Swiss boarding school in the outskirts of a town called St. Gallen, which *Nonno* had chosen for her "education".

For the past few months, the relationship between father and daughter had become unbearable: Mia was at an age in which teens do not give a hoot who their parents are or what they stand for. *Nonno* was an internationally known architect, who had decided that he had had enough of her wild ways and was no longer going to tolerate her attitude.

She was busy scribbling on a piece of paper, when to her right a latecomer arrived, slamming her bag on the table beside hers. The girl looked very flustered and, most of all, very angry. They looked at each other for a split second and Mia immediately felt her guts calming down. It was Charlotte. Another half-hour of torture went by, but as soon as the bell rang and all the dumbbells rushed out the door, Mia felt a tugging at her sleeve.

"Shall we have a cigarette?" said Charlotte, "This is my first day in this hell-hole; what foul luck brought you here?"

Mia had never smoked before, except with Livia, her childhood best friend since they were seven; they had vomited and then gotten whipped by the maid.

"It's also my first day. But let's have that cigarette!" she answered, following Charlotte out the door all the way to the back of the building. The latter then pulled out a packet of Lucky Strikes and lit one up, clearly showing that was not her first smoke.

"Don't you have yours?" she said, blowing smoke straight into Mia's face.

"No, sorry, I forgot mine at home," Mia lied, practically choking on Charlotte's smoke.

22

"Here you go, girl! I'm a sharer! So, what's your story?" Charlotte asked, point blank.

On the opposite side of the building, as Mia was about to answer, they both heard and then saw another group of kids coming their way. A red-haired, freckle-face, pretty boy and a black-haired "pocket Venus" (Mia's expression for a small beauty), were heading towards them, both holding cigarettes in their hands, as if they were wielding weapons.

"Hey, what's up new girls? Aah... already smoking! My name is Isabella." Pocket Venus was the first to speak.

"Isabella, look at these two beauties... what a great addition to the club!" Freckle-Face added.

"Where're you from, little birds?" Isabella enquired.

"I don't know where you're from, but I know where you're going to end up!" Freckle-Face, said with a smirk, pointing at his penis.

He was unable to finish his sentence as Charlotte promptly zonked him across the face.

"Shiiiittttttt!" he cursed, bleeding from the nose, while groping on the floor, trying to pick up the cigarette that had flown from his mouth. Isabella was laughing her head off, Mia terrified and Charlotte was more than ready to box him again.

"Freckle-Face", whose real name was François Vareppe, looked up at the three girls. He was clearly humiliated and blurted out a few insults at them before disappearing in the direction of the toilet to wash away his embarrassment.

A short distance away, a lovely blonde, another "new kid", was looking on at the entire scene with a smile slowly mountain-climbing across her face. It was Lena, who then walked up to them and introduced herself. All four would become inseparable, and The Rosenberg Boarding School "prison" slowly but surely turned into their new home. This was going to be remembered as the first encounter of the forever-lasting friendship, which ever after would be known as "The Witches".

NEW YORK CITY – 2005, The Vernissage

The sun's rays poured right through the window, the curtains had been left open, inundating Mia's bed with a feeling of warmth and bliss. It was as if she were both sunbathing and recharging her spent energies, a glorious morning full of possibilities and endless opportunities! It was the D-Day: Mia's first solo show. "The Opening" (the name she had chosen for the big event). She needed to get ready, both physically and psychologically. Louis was expecting her at 4 p.m. to meet some so-called VIPs and she needed to "get her face on". The morning routine was always the same: a cup of coffee and that nasty-looking and equally nasty-tasting orange vitamin drink.

The difference this morning was that her apartment was nice and tidy, and this made her feel somehow more respectable and worthy of herself.

She switched on Radio Italia News. Although she would not necessarily pay attention to all that was said, hearing her mother tongue relaxed her and gave her a much-needed sense of security. Suddenly, she caught the tail end of a news item that struck her entire being, as if she'd been hit by lightning: there had been an earthquake in Umbria. She could not believe her ears. How come no one had called? Suddenly the memories of the 1997's tragedy filled her head. It was all still so fresh in her mind.

She rushed to the phone and frantically dialed home.

"*Maman*?!"

"Mia, *ma chérie,* is it you?"

"Yes, *Maman*, it's me! My God, I just heard the news, are you okay?"

"Yes, *Tesoro.* All is fine, thankfully. The house shook and we all ran outside but nothing like what happened in 1997... I'm sure you remember?"

"Yes, *Maman*, I remember, of course. Oh! I am so relieved, thank God. I will call Livia now to check on her. It's just that today, well, you know, it's my *vernissage* at Louis's gallery. Do you remember Louis?"

"Oh, yes, I remember him. Oh good! Your *vernissage*? You didn't tell me you were preparing a show. That's fantastic! I wish I was there, but then again, you know how much I hate New York. Too many bad memories for me there..."

"Yes, *Maman*, I know. Memories are not easy for me either. Well, listen, I got to go now. *Bisous, Maman*"

"*Bisous, ma chérie.*"

Conversations between Mia and *Maman* had always either lasted two seconds or two hours. Her relationship with her parents had never been an easy-going affair, all the more so after my departure. Mia had been the rebellious type since day one. After two previous marriages and much older children from their first beds, her parents were not necessarily strict with Mia. However, they had still been rather censuring.

She had grown up in what was considered (and still is) a modern-looking house, not far from the ancient town of Assisi. Her father, a renowned Swiss architect had met my grandmother while on a visit to Umbria with his students from the *Ecole Polytechnique Fédérale de Lausanne (EPFL).* It was *coup de foudre.* Proof of this

25

was the "Mausoleum" he had built for his nascent family on a hill, with a clear view of the surrounding beautiful landscape. As a child, she had been given the nickname *La Svizzera* by her friends as well as the locals, and it stuck to her throughout her adolescence, even if she was Italian. But this did not bother her in the least. In fact, she liked to attract attention to herself. And boy, did she get attention! The mixture of her choleric father's "strange house", coupled with the freedom she was given very early on, made her a strange and different creature in the eyes of her sleepy town's populace. Kids loved her alright, but very often, parents did not appreciate their children hanging around such a *strana ragazza.*

Her best friend, Livia, lived on the hill across hers, and whenever she looked back on her childhood, she felt it had been a privileged life, full of happiness and joy, even if there had been dark patches here and there. Do we not so often remember the good things and forget all that is unpleasant? As the daughters of somewhat older parents (the latter were over forty when Livia and Mia were born), they were left to themselves most of the time. The two of them would meet midway between their two hills and sit under their favorite olive tree whenever "things" with their respective parents did not run smoothly. They looked like angels, but were two little rascals who would paint kittens for the fun of it; climb rooftops like tomboys, disappear during the Venice Biennale and even when a little older, hitchhike their way to Rimini to see a Jovanotti concert without telling a soul. They pledged eternal friendship, and so it was.

She again picked up the phone and rang her favorite friend.

"Livia, *Pulce? Come stai?"*

"Mia! *Pulce*… what a fucking nightmare. We were so scared… remember 1997?"

"*Sì, sì,* Livia, I remember. Are you okay? The family? The house?"

"Yes, all okay, just a few tiles which fell from the roof of the barn, but nothing more. *Che paura*! How are you doing?"

"I'm fine, all's well… Listen, I need to rush, just wanted to check up on you."

"*Grazie pulce. Sì, tutto bene,* don't worry. *Bacio.*"

"*Bacio.*"

The incredible thing about their friendship was that a few words between them sufficed. No long explanations were required. These two knew each other so well that, like soulmates, they could practically communicate through space and time without uttering a word. Even if years elapsed without seeing each other, the moment they got together it was as if time had never moved forward. That indeed must be the meaning of true friendship. Unlike Mia, Livia had chosen to stay in Italy. She had always known who she was and what she wanted; there was no need for her to cross any river, sea, ocean, or lake. Livia was special. Unique.

The Witches were special too, but in a different, more carefree manner. Mia was thrilled that they would be at her side tonight, on such a special occasion. With them, there was always a story to tell – something happening, psychodramas, bad-boy experiences, tarot-card reader's advice to follow… No matter what or where, their meetings and venues were always accompanied by excessive quantities of champagne and gin tonic.

Once again, she realized that time was not giving her respite. She quickly put on her trainers and headed out to have her "face put on" a session which always proved to be an extremely painful experience for both her and whoever was the unlucky person in charge of trying, with the best will in the world, to do it!

4:00 p.m.

There she was. Standing beside Louis, in the middle of the gallery, ready to meet and greet the six journalists who had come to interview her. Her new black dress now felt too small and her pantyhose as if it were about to roll down her legs. She had lost her favorite hair clip and wished desperately that she could smoke. The champagne had not yet arrived – *arghhhhh*! Only glasses of water with lemon zest, accompanied by celery and carrot sticks were being served. In short: none of this boded well and Mia was on edge.

Louis was the chatting-type and was soon engrossed in a long-winded explanation about Mia's work. She stood by, ready to reply in the most polite, obsequious manner to their queries. Big words kept pouring out of their learned mouths and she felt like a total hypocrite, making it all up as she went along, trying to sound as sincere and honest as possible. Why must artists explain their art? Aren't there "experts" who do just that and nothing else?

Good thing Louis was there and enjoyed this. He was in his element. It seemed to her that the journalists saw many things in her work that in no way corresponded to what had inspired her. Her work had been created in a daze, under a creative spell that was hard to put into words. How could they possibly understand, let alone like, what she did, when for her it was a painful, but necessary, cathartic, experience?

Mia needed a thick skin to move about and come out unscarred from the load of hypocrisy (and plain crap) that was thrown in all directions. The question was, how could she maintain a clean, innocent soul, and create beautiful work, without being tainted by the money, the power and the egos that were everywhere? There was and is nothing pretty in this so-called "art-world".

Mia was full of these and other thoughts as she felt time move at a snail's-pace: minutes felt like hours and all that she could think of was getting the hell out of there. A young man with a tray-full of glasses of water appeared out of nowhere and she grabbed one. She chewed on the lemon zest with such eagerness that she bit her tongue – *ouchhhhhhh!* She clearly needed a drink. Anything! In her distress, she turned around and looked in the direction of the bar to see if there was any kind of alcohol: *Nada, Niente, Nichts, Rien de Rien…*

Linda, who wrote the art column in *Time Out* seemed to be having the time of her life, chatting away with Louis; Jessica from *Art News* was taking pictures for her blog; Chao from *NYArts* was also taking pictures, and Lesley from the *New York Magazine* was heading towards her.

"Mia, congratulations for the show. I'm impressed!"

"Thank you, that's very kind of you. Would you care for a glass of water with a celery or carrot stick?"

"Yes, please!"

'Goodness gracious, this woman is excited about a carrot stick!' Mia thought.

"So, how long have you been working on the show, and how is the family?"

Argh… Not *That* Question! Thankfully, she was rescued in the moment of panic by The Witches, who waltzed through the door, looking like crazy fairies on their high heels and in their tight jeans bearing beaming smiles.

Charlotte was the first to shout out:

"MIA! Come over here darling, let's give you some love!"

"Hurrah!!!! Yessssss! Charlotte, what's in that big bag of yours?"

"Ha! Come and get it! It's a parcel filled with special potions for you!"

Mia smiled politely to Louis's "VIPs" and ran to her friends. She was ecstatic to hug them and feel their craziness enveloping her! Together they ran to the toilet...

"My babies! I'm so fucking happy you're here!"

"Little bird," screeched Isabella, "Do you need a drink or a shrink?"

"You're looking way too serious," Lena added. "Have some of our secret potion!"

A few minutes later they reappeared, wearing a little too much make-up, and what the hell was that little powder sticking out of Isabella's nose? Ah! They didn't give a damn. They were together, that's all that counted. And this *vernissage* in New York was a damn good reason to party!

Mia and The Witches were all incredibly fun and loving; however, from my vantage point, I could clearly sense Mia's profound unease. If I were only able to whisper into her ear, "I love you, please don't worry". But this was not possible, and neither could she hear Louis murmuring that she should tell her friends to mellow and join him in promoting the show, because in the end that's what counted. Louis had decided to sell Mia's pain: The "dead-daughter-card", as Mia would call it. He kept blurting out banalities, such as "troubled souls always produce great works", or "from Bacon, to Basquiat, to Bambi!" (This last one being his favorite for some weird reason that nobody really understood). Finally, the drinks arrived!

The *vernissage* lasted for a few hours; the Witches spent the evening outside the gallery, drinking, laughing and smoking. Dad and Marco came by to say hello but didn't stay for long. This most probably because Dad couldn't stand Mia's work and was mumbling that she had copied him!

Around 7 p.m., my favorite person in the world walked in with his family, along with a few nurses from the Sloan Kettering Cancer Center: it was my hero, Dr. Diraf. My Diraf. Mia flushed, beaming with happiness. Of all people, he was the one who had devoted more hours, energy and effort to fighting my illness. He had been by my side, night and day, caring for me like no one else. He had gone beyond the call of duty, and I believe that he did so out of love. He was a compassionate and caring man, and I'll be grateful to him till the end of time.

The evening turned out to be a success. Mia socialized and was attentive to one and all (no doubt the magic potion had done the trick). At closure time, ninety percent of the pieces had been sold and Louis was euphoric. He and Mia closed the gallery, shook hands like two tennis players at the end of a long, exhausting match. Still, she could not help feeling like an impostor, as if she had sold her soul to the devil. And yet, she had succeeded; she had done it! She could now boast of being a recognized and respected sculptor who had something to add to the cultural scene of that great metropolis that was New York! A place where one either perished or succeeded, but never languished in limbo. But the price she had paid had been a great one: despite the fact that she had crossed an ocean and become someone recognized by many, somewhere along the way of this vital adventure, she had lost what was most precious to her. This wound was deep and would take years to heal, if heal it must.

As she walked in search of a cab, the *beeping* sound, which for many months had drilled a hole in her head and in her spirit and had been a source of anxiety during so many wakeful nights, suddenly began to fill her ears. Was her drunken brain messing with her head once more? Again?

She was, thankfully, brought back to the present by her phone ringing. It was Hermès, who was now outside her apartment where he had last parted with his missing tie, which he seemed to need at this most ungodly hour.

"Jesus, man! Do you really need that ugly tie? Just ring the bell and my friends will let you in," Mia blurted out.

MIDNIGHT IN THE CITY

It had been a long time coming: the money, being "semi-famous" and all that this entailed. For years, she had struggled, sometimes even having to count the coins that would pay for the subway ride to take her to her waitressing job in the city. She could now envisage the true possibility of going home to Italy for the summer holidays with Marco, and take Livia somewhere chic for a few days. As she crossed the bridge for the second time in less than twenty-four hours, this time around she was lighthearted. With the cab's windows completely rolled down, speeding across the deserted city, she laughed out loud thinking of The Witches terrorizing Hermès at home!

Meanwhile, elsewhere, the intercom to her apartment had just been buzzed:

"Hello!? Who is it?" screeched a woman with a broken Irish accent.

34

"Good evening, I am Mia's friend. I came by to pick up something of mine."

"Come on in. Let me know if I've managed to open the door..."

As he walked up the stairs, he could hear music coming from Mia's floor. It was bad enough that he had had to come all the way back into Brooklyn; but having to climb up the steps gave him the absolute creeps. He had heard Billy Idol blasting down the street as he'd approached the building, and now as he entered, it boomed throughout the stairs. What on earth was going on? As he reached the landing, he noticed the door open and knocked hesitantly before entering. The Witches were dancing frantically, as if in the trance or in some sort of ritual and didn't even notice his presence.

"In the midnight hour she cried more, more, more...with a rebel yell, more, more, more, more, more, more..." they all sang, or screamed and screeched (to be honest), accompanying the music. Then, all of a sudden, they caught sight of him: tall, blond, green eyes, extremely well dressed in a pearl-gray, three-piece tailored suit.

"Umhum... So, you're Mia's friend..."

"Yes, that's right... I'm so sorry to break in like this and interrupt your singing. I just need to pick something up... I think I left it here... maybe it's in Mia's room."

"Well, Mia isn't here at the moment... Why not wait for her and, in the meantime, you join us for a drink. By the way, my name is Charlotte."

Hermès took off his jacket. He was beginning to be intrigued. He had finished work hours ago and this sounded like the best invitation he had received in a while.

By the time Mia arrived, Hermès, Isabella and Charlotte were making out on the couch.

"What the fuck?" she snarled on seeing the scene.

They ignored her altogether and carried on groping each other and although she felt as hot as a red chili pepper and all that she could think of was lashing out at them, she instead forced herself to calm down, brush her teeth, grab the weed box and slip into her bedroom (with a big glass of water). She closed the door behind her. Lena was sleeping on her bed. She had always been the "good one" of the group.

The curtains were wide open, the way Mia liked it. She actually loved her room. It was her nest, the place she felt safest of all. The white sheets smelled beautifully clean. The simplicity of this space cleared her mind. But above all, it was the view that was most soothing to her. This view and the changing light, depending on the season and time of day.

Puerto Rican music was spilling out of the restaurant below and the subway could be heard rattling ahead. She was alive! She rolled herself a big fat spliff and tried to wake Lena up: impossible, she was sound asleep. She was lucky, she could fall asleep wherever she was if her body was in need of rest. No matter what was taking place around her, be it a party or people coming and going, Lena could just shut her eyes and sleep and then wake up rested and ready to carry on with the fun.

Mia slid open the window and watched the smoke drifting through the air. The hot smoke penetrated her entire body and she slowly felt relaxed and relieved that her day had come to an end. Finally, she was free of the incessant anxiety that she had learnt to live with most of the time.

THE RADIATOR

She woke up the following morning to an apartment turned upside down by The Witches, exactly as she had expected. Thankfully, Hermès was gone. The Witches were fast asleep on the sofa. Lena, of course, was awake. She had already bought breakfast, was making coffee, and grumbling about the mess. It was 9 a.m. – perhaps a bit too early to get started! Mia decided to slip back into bed, but as she was about to do so, the phone rang. *'Damn it!'* – telephones, always creeping into our lives and intruding, she thought. If it hadn't been for Marco, she wouldn't have answered. Hopefully, this would be short.

"Ciao Mia. *Bravo pour ton expo...* I just wanted to congratulate you for last night."

It was *Nonno* (my grandfather) who was calling her for the first time since he had decided a few years back to ignore her altogether. Unbelievable, he had finally called her; her heart skipped a beat.

"Papa? *Ça va?* Did you see my works?"

"*Maman* told me to call you. She's so proud of you."

"Aha, *merci...* how are you?"

"Fine, *ti passo maman...*"

Mia hung up.

Mia was the youngest of five. *Nonno* had always called her *la prediletta,* but that was years ago. So far back that it seemed that it was in some other life. The smell of his pipe animated all of her childhood memories of him as did the feel of his cold jackets when he came home from work on late autumn evenings. It was more about "theory" with *Nonno* and less about the "facts". Mia loved to challenge and contradict him; little did she imagine that one day he would simply – and without any explanation – decide to stop loving her. His abruptness had once again thrown her off balance right into an open wound. One which in all these years had not healed but festered. God only knows how much Mia missed her father. I felt so bad for her and so did The Witches. They were now looking at her wide awake. They knew what was coming: reality, like a thunderbolt, was racing straight to her heart and would beat her to the ground like a tree struck by lightning. Next, Mia was holding onto the radiator with all her strength, like a castaway holds onto a buoy so as not to drown.

This was a déjà-vu.

The morning I departed, while the nurses and doctors were trying to bring me back, Mia was on the floor, feeling like a worm, in a corner of the room holding onto a radiator as if it had supernatural powers and could bring me back to her side. At the time, the lovely nurses could do nothing for her, except pour blue pills into her mouth. They were her friends and my Angels. By the time Dad arrived, I was already well into the light. He tried, but was unable to pry her free from the damn radiator. Dr. Diraf walked in and slowly approached Mia who was latched onto the radiator, as if letting go of it meant sinking to the bottom of the ocean.

"Mia... Mia... *C'est moi*, Dr. Diraf..." He tried to reassure her, as he had done for the past few months, but this time around he knew that there were no more plans or protocols.

I was gone. He too was crying; everyone was in tears, with Mia attached to the radiator.

Dr. Diraf gently took her hand and in silence pried it from the contraption that had become Mia's succor and putting all the emphasis and strength into his voice, he said:

"Mia! I'm so sorry. We are all so sorry."

Mia slowly calmed down, she stood up, right in front of Dr. Diraf, who had not let go of her hand, and stared right into his eyes. On the other side of the room, Dad was talking to the nurses – was she in a dream? Another one of her nightmares? No, this was real... Mia, who still held onto Dr. Diraf's hand, slowly approached Dad. Meanwhile, I lay in my little bed.

A cold body in pink pajamas.

Dad and Mia were unable to look into each other's eyes. Their mouths were unable to utter a word – both were breathless, exhausted, totally spent. But there was still one last hurdle they had to go through: they had to say goodbye. Never had I seen so heart-wrenching a scene as that of my parents seeing me off. Finally, Mia let go of Dr. Diraf's hand. She walked out of the room in which we had been best roommates for so many months and did not look back. She stepped inside the elevator, which stopped on the sixth floor. People came in and she just looked at them as if in a numb cloud. The lift continued down to the ground floor, she exited the hospital, and walked out the sliding doors. Outside the magnolia trees were in full blossom.

Infinite beauty is a will-o'-the-wisp.

MARCO

A few hours later, with The Witches help, Mia had pulled herself together. The gallery champagne brunch was finally over; the last drops had been licked clean from out of the bottom of the glasses. The Witches were now ready to head back to the airport. Their presence was – as it always was – short, but intense.

By 8 p.m. everything had fallen back into place: her apartment, her fridge, her washing… Everything, except a few pieces of her life. Marco would be coming home the next day to spend the entire week with her. Finally, this time around they would have a good time, she promised herself, without any kind of misunderstandings or tense moments. She switched on her favorite radio programme and listened to the latest news on the Italian earthquake. A brief, but heartwarming, exchange with Livia followed. Hungover and drained Mia longed for her Umbrian hills more than ever. Outside the streets were packed with rushing cars and people. It seemed as if New York never came up for air, it was a constant non-stop locomotive of frantic activity. For a split second, she wondered if the moment hadn't come for her to leave, to move to another city, relocate. But where? With whom? And to do what? No, it was best to stay put… at least for now; it was time to hit the sack alone – and rest.

The following morning, as she approached Dad's apartment, she noticed that Marco was already waiting for her on the sidewalk. Dad was looking down from the window and waving goodbye to both of them. As they waved back, Mia thought to herself that she wished she had spared some extra minutes of conversation: it would have been a good way to start the day.

On the way to school, Marco bombarded her with questions regarding the show, The Witches, Louis… He wanted to know everything. He was a curious child, full of life and now that I was gone, she had to redouble her love for my brother. For her own sanity, if nothing else.

According to Isabella, my brother Marco is, without any doubt, an Indigo child. At least this is what she used to tell Mia whenever she complained that his school grades were poor.

Marco is incredibly smart; he simply never had the patience to learn. His teachers would say that he was bright but could not concentrate. He often ended up in the headmaster's office because of his "disruptive" behavior. However, he was intelligent and full of empathy for others, for his parents, and for me. He loved me so much and always looked at me with bewilderment and awe as if I was some sort of extraterrestrial being that had landed from out of space. Marco was now spending half of his time with Mia and the other half with Dad. Jules was also living with Dad. As Mia filled Marco with kisses at the school entrance, they agreed to meet at that exact same spot at 6 p.m. after school.

Considering it was only 9 a.m., Mia decided that she should (and would!) have enough time to go back to bed before meeting Louis for lunch. It was time to talk about money! But nothing ever went as expected in Mia's life, as you may have divined by now and by the time she reached home, she found Hermès waiting for her on the front step.

He was in his trainers; he'd probably forgotten something again. Somewhat surprised and expectant, Mia smiled upon seeing him.

"I'm sorry about the other night, Mia. I'm never sure what your feelings are for me. I do not know where I stand. How long do you want to go on like this?"

"I don't know, I'm not quite sure what you're talking about?"

"*Je t'adore, Mia, mais j'en peux plus.*" And as quickly as he had appeared, he was gone. No booty call for Mia this morning!

Dommage!

The only thing left for her to do was to get an additional couple of hours sleep before meeting Louis. Enough tears shed for the week, the time had come to get at least two answers: "How much did we sell last night?" and, "Do you think we could have a second Bloody Mary?"

She fell asleep right away, but it wasn't long before the phone rang.

'SHITTTTTT! What the hell?!...'

By the time she reached the phone, the message had been left: it was Louis confirming that he had reserved a table at the Gramercy Tavern for 1 p.m. This was a good sign: it meant sales had gone well.

PART II

UMBRIA – 1991, Mia and Dad

The day Dad walked into his first real job; Mia was busy at work inside the biggest sculpture studio he had ever seen. She was dressed in a plaster-covered *salopette*, scrubbing a twelve-meter-high Styrofoam column, holding something which looked like a huge carrot scraper. This was to be the cast-iron sculpture which would eventually stand on Central Park in N.Y.

Mia saw him (and his friend) from out of the corner of her eye but was hardly going to make contact or a fuss over the two young men. Although, it must be said, they had been recommended by the best art school in Italy, while she, Mia, had been working and learning the hard way with Meredith, the latter's sixty-five-year-old studio assistant, Milton, and Bruna the cook. Her favorite words being *"Dio cane"* and *"Madonna tisica"* (Holy Dog and Phthisic Madonna, respectively). Bruna, who barked instead of talking, had unexpectedly taken a liking to Mia. She shared and taught her secret Umbrian recipes about olive trees, wild chicory, and many others.

Mia was twenty at the time and needed to prove that she could work and learn quicker and harder than anyone else. Meredith had agreed to "adopt" her the day that she had found her, aged fifteen, sitting outside her studio, begging to be of use. Grandpapa, my grandfather, had kicked her out of the house a few hours earlier, and all she had to her name was a fake US driver's license, a red Alfa Romeo, and a one-hundred-and-eighty-tree olive grove.

45

Meredith was a tough cookie: a Jewish-American artist of great renown who had settled in Italy in the early 50s and had forged herself a career in the unforgiving, macho world of art. She neither minced her words or beat about the bush and knew exactly who that girl standing in front of her was. She looked straight into Mia's eyes said:

"No more bullshit, Mia. If you want to be here, you will work your ass off." And added, "Your parents are imbeciles and in spite of the fact that I love you, you'll still have to fight to make me like you."

The artists who had chosen to live on these luscious rolling hills were incredibly gifted, sometimes famous and quite often riotous. They would meet around good food, wine, and interminable discussions, and in time would put this Umbrian outpost on the map of international art. Mia felt it in her bones that this was the right place for her, no matter how hard working for Meredith would turn out to be. She knew, deep down, that there was no better school than this one.

As Meredith approached her with the two young men, Mia immediately noticed there was something quite unique about the taller one (Dad). Rarely had she sensed so much strength and fragility combined. They were introduced briefly, and as Meredith was leading the two young men to the other side of the studio, Dad hurried back to Mia, who was now forced to stop what she was doing and look up. She knew that Meredith would be furious if this exchange weren't swift. Up close, Mia realized that he was different: his eyes pierced right through her, and she felt as if her knees were about to buckle.

"*Sei bellissima e lascerò tutto per te se me lo permetti,*" Dad blurted out, taken by mother's rough, animal-like attractiveness.

Mia could see that his body language meant every word that he had uttered, and she swooned, filled with a passionate intensity like she'd never felt before. He was for real; his eyes had looked at her as though Zorro had found someone to save or as if Garfield had discovered lasagna! In her heart, she prayed that Meredith had not overheard him. Those simple, yet heartfelt words, stuck to the studio's roof for days, weeks, and months. Something unknown, different, fresh, authentic, had touched her heart. They soon became colleagues, then friends – never forgetting that first encounter. The friendship matured into passion, sex, and finally... love.

Their first kiss took place while on assignment. They were driving Meredith's truck, carrying huge Styrofoam pieces of Meredith's. Dad was sweating in a disgusting-looking *canottiera*, all worried that they would arrive to the foundry without breaking. All of a sudden, as they were driving along, a big block of Styrofoam fell out of the truck!

"*Porca Madonna!*" they both shouted in unison.

They pulled over and were soon able to retrieve the piece from out of the middle of the highway, where it was lying. It was a hot, humid day, and after dragging the piece of Styrofoam off the road, they caught their breath resting against it on the side of the highway, a bundle of nerves, when suddenly without a second thought or any premeditated idea, they turned around, faced each other and as if hypnotized, drew closer and closer, till their lips touched and melted into a long, passionate kiss. It was their first kiss and would be the beginning of a long, steaming affair.

From that day onwards, they made love whenever and wherever they could: on top of sculptures, in Meredith's bed, inside the red Alfa Romeo, and under the olive trees. Their bodies seemed to be made for each other, a perfect fit, like two well-oiled pieces of machinery which functioned in perfect harmony. They would go for long car rides in Mia's red Alfa Romeo, listening to music and weaving dreams and plans for a future full of magic and hope. When Dad drove, she would place her hand under his leg: they were inseparable and curiously dependent on one another.

They continued working with Meredith in the huge studio, drinking Campari in the morning, living for their love for art, happy and hopeful for an inseparable life together.

One night, after they had been out carousing till late, Dad proposed. He told Mia that he had known he wanted to marry her the very instant he had laid his eyes on her and had considered her his wife after their first kiss. That night, with tears of drunken joy in her eyes, Mia accepted. Nine months later, my brother Marco arrived. Neither one had ever been happier. It was pure bliss and the future was so full of possibilities that nothing, no one, could have come between them and their future.

MARRIED LIFE

There is a saying in Italy: *"Sposa bagnata, sposa fortunata!"* and the day that my parents got married it rained. But for some odd reason, Mia had a strange premonition that that saying might not always be accurate. Their wedding night could not have been more romantic: full of laughter, color, flowers, and festivities

48

till the very early hours of the morning. The following day's hangover was as memorable as the occasion called for.

My brother Marco, who had not yet turned one, slept between them in their big bed. Faithful Jules was as always at their side. Notwithstanding the fact that Marco woke them up at 5 a.m., the following day was a very happy one. Love was like a magic potion: it warded off all evil.

However, it must be said that my grandparents always had their reservations and were apprehensive regarding my parents' relationship and the communication between both families was practically non-existent. The wedding had brought together two separate universes and they knew full well that theirs was not a common destiny. Our household was a happy one. Lively day and night. Mia's passion for cooking meant that there was always a smell of delicious food floating in the air. A fire constantly burnt in the kitchen: we would grill meat, fish, and vegetables, tempting friends and neighbours to show up almost every evening to join the fun. It goes without saying that during these evenings lots of unlabeled, acidy, local wine was drunk.

When spring came around, everyone would be ready to pick wild asparagus to make *spaghetti alla boscaiola* and *frittata* with eggs laid by Bruna's hens. Summertime meant all sorts of fantastic home-grown vegetables – *Panzanella* made with their tomatoes and basil, stuffed eggplant, *mozzarella di bufala* and *prosciutto e melone...* In the autumn, it was mushrooms hunting-time: *porcini, ovuli...* and once in a while, on memorable days, truffles would make their appearance on our table. What great days these were!

November was Mia's favorite time of the year: it meant olive picking and producing olive oil from her precious trees. It was a week-long affair, and everyone was involved: children, men, women, young and old. This was a tradition, an intrinsic part of their Umbrian culture. She would take time off from Meredith's studio and, along with Marco who was all wrapped in blankets and would be left lying on the grass while she would pick the olives along with friends and local farmers. Nets were installed under the trees at dawn and the olives were knocked off as quickly as possible so that the humidity would not sink into the little green and black fruit. It was often cold and foggy and by no means an easy job, although all had a great time. Everyone brought some kind of specialty – homemade wine, bread, cheese or salami – and they would take breaks trying each other's produce. When all the olives were picked, they would load them into a friend's *Apetto* and bring them to the *frantoio*. They often spent the night there, watching as the oil was extracted, tasting it on bread grilled on the embers of the *frantoio's* fireplace. It was a carefree life, full of wonder and magic; simple yet filled with poetry and bliss.

I wonder when and why Mom and Dad stopped adoring each other as in the beginning. What went wrong? What was it that made their relationship unravel like a ball of yarn?

NEW YORK – 1996, Brooklyn! *Il futuro!*

In January, Meredith decided she needed them both in her New York studio. The move was quick, fun, and exciting. Little did they know that that gargantuan city would chew them up and spit them out as it had so many others before them. New York brought out the best and worst in them. Expectations were running high, for both of them. Before long, Dad would find himself a new nest – not exactly the kind of nest Mia had envisaged.

"*Broooklyn! Il futuro!*" Those were Dad's words.

How prescient they turned out to be, but again, for all the wrong reasons. But let us not get ahead of ourselves. When Mia first set sight on what would become their new home – as she got off the J train on the Brooklyn Broadway Line – there was a huge graffiti that read: "The House of Death" painted on the front door.

Dad, who was an amazing craftsman, and could repair anything, washed off the graffiti, repainted the door and skilfully built what was going to be their great loft in the ex-crack house. They had very little money, however, between Dad's ingenuity and mother's thriftiness, they could, and did, work miracles when they set their hearts to it. The loft was filled with light! Marco's bedroom was facing the subway tracks while the back stairs were overlooking the *projects*. Jules loved to slip out the back window and pretend he was standing up against the neighbor's mean-looking Pit Bulls (honestly, in truth, all he sought was acceptance; being one of the gang).

It's worth pointing out that they were considered part of the early "settlers": the first Caucasian family living on Broadway, amid Puerto Ricans and Hasidic Jews. Their loft building was so close to the subway line that, whenever the subway rattled passed them, if they were carrying on a conversation, they had to stop talking because otherwise they couldn't hear one another. In time, however, they got used to it. Mia and Dad turned out to be excellent superintendents and ran a tight ship. And what used to be a crack house soon became a quaint four-story building known throughout the neighborhood as "The Family" eventually housing painters, filmmakers, photographers, and other non-descript artists of various hues at any hour of the day or night, doors were flung open and music and people came and went in what was to become my future home.

These were crazy and beautiful times. An orgy of art, drugs and ambition that Mia and Dad indulged in equal amounts. There was not much sense trying to make heads or tails of it all; of what the future held in store for them, or even time to plan for it. It was a matter of living the present and making the most of it. Carpe diem.

THE FAMILY

At the beginning Dad and Mia worked for Meredith as planned, trying to make ends meet. New York was an expensive city and, moreover, Dad started having bad habits that soon got the better of him. All the same, they were still convinced that they were in the right place at the right time. They were committed to making it.

When Meredith wasn't in town, her middle-aged Indian cleaning lady came during the day to take care of Marco, so that Mia and Dad could work in Meredith's Tribeca studio. When in the mood, she'd clean up the loft, but for the most part, she read the Bible out loud to herself and to my brother, who no doubt was clueless as to what she was mumbling. When Meredith was in town, the middle-aged Indian cleaning-lady's niece replaced her.

Often, after a long day working in the studio, Dad would go home and Mia would head out to her "real job", which most of the time never finished before 1 a.m. She either bartended, waitressed and once even managed an

S&M club. Mia would take whatever she was offered, as long as it paid decent wages. Dad, for his part, would take time to play with Marco, and the middle-aged Indian cleaning lady's niece was often home, too, to make sure Dad and Marco would not spend their evenings alone.

There began to be more and more arguments between Dad and Mia, their shouts became part of the "The Family", but sooner or later they would finish in bed, making love. Whenever arguments broke out at work, Meredith would mediate between the two of them, but deep down all that she really cared about was to make sure they got their work done and could concentrate on her latest (and always) important projects. She could not afford to waste time on what seemed to her petty conflicts. In truth, she had never been a fan of this relationship, far from it. On good days, Mia and Dad laughed about the fact that she was jealous, and on bad days, Mia yelled and yelled that she should have listened to her mentor mother figure Meredith. It seemed as if New York was slowly gobbling them down like a giant monster listening to the Chemical Brothers, but there was more to it. Unlike Dad, Mia had never been the "real artist" in the family. She felt that there might be more in her: a space, an energy, which could go beyond simply looking after Dad and Meredith. Mia's mom had always told her that she was a special child. Unfortunately, *Nonno's* egocentric, bright, narcissistic, manipulating personality had stymied her budding confidence. In a nutshell: her parents had not helped her build any type of self-esteem; Meredith and Dad had proved no better.

Mia dreamt of working for herself, having a show of her own, selling her creations and ultimately, living off the profits of her work. She needed a plan and time. Most of all, she needed to believe in herself. Secretly – whilst lying to everyone that she was bartending – she had signed up for evening classes at the Parsons School of Design. At first, it was a frightening experience, but after a few weeks she became comfortable with her new secret friends (the other pupils). Most of all, she had access to the school's studio which, if she wanted, she could use any time, day or night. Three years had gone by amid fights, parties, and the simple act of surviving, and one night, unbeknownst to all, my father's little seed landed into Mia's belly. For the first few months, life ran its course. Mia was particularly grumpy and tired and Dad was staying out of the way as much as possible. It was only when Mia, on her fourth month of pregnancy went for a check-up, that she learned about my existence. My parents were young and the future was still full of possibilities. This piece of unexpected news encouraged Dad to finally find a real money-making job, away from the studio, which he did, in a company based out of New Jersey, a two-hour drive from N.Y.

For a while, it seemed as if family life had finally cooled everyone's heads and spread a soothing balm over our lives. A month later it was official: I'd be a girl, their minds and hearts burst with happiness!

WINTER 2000

It was an extremely cold and harsh winter, but beautiful. There seemed to be no end to the falling snow. The gray abandoned factories along the Williamsburg side of the river were covered in a pristine white mantle. It all looked like a beautiful ghost industrial archeological site.

At the time, Mia did not have as much work with Meredith so, she would take my brother for long walks along Broadway, under the train tracks, all the way to the waterfront overlooking Manhattan. Jules would accompany us, running wild, appearing and disappearing from out the piles of snow that were formed on the sides of the townhouses that we passed. Williamsburg was only beginning to be gentrified and a few little diners welcomed Mia and us for coffee or a glass of wine at the end of the day.

Dad's late hours became a rule together with Mia's burning jealousy. This was Mia's second pregnancy, and although she was happy and excited about my coming, she could not accept the way in which her body was changing. Dad hardly looked at her, let alone touched her. She longed to be kissed, caressed, and slowly and painfully shut herself up, with a feeling of despondency and loneliness. Most nights, Mia would come back home late from work, but for some reason, on that particular night, she was home much earlier than expected.

As she tiptoed in, trying to make as little noise as possible, she heard the shower tap running. Dad, she thought to herself. A few years earlier, she would have quickly undressed to join him, but that was then... Instead, she took off her wet coat, kicked her shoes into a corner, and headed to the kitchen. She switched the electric kettle on, pulled a cup from the cupboard, and looked out the kitchen window while waiting for the water to boil. She then heard the shower tap close as she was preparing herself a chamomile. The bathroom door opened; a female's giggling voice broke the silence; her footsteps heading down the corridor towards the kitchen, followed by a second person's footsteps. A moment later, the cleaning lady's niece stood in one of Mia's robes, drying her hair with a towel, Dad's naked body right behind, clinging onto hers. It was as if she had been punched in the stomach, knocking the wind out of her, and as she gasped, the chamomile cup slipped out of her hand, falling onto the floor, and shattering into smithereens. It was as if the room were sucking all three of them up, with their faces growing and shrinking by moments. Seconds ticked away as if they were hours.

Screams, yelling, commotion. Several neighbors rushed to our door to see what the matter was, only to find the not-so-nice niece and Dad standing naked by the door's entrance. They had been locked out. Thankfully, Marco, who was a heavy sleeper, had not heard a thing.

Mia locked herself inside the loft. Lying on the front room's floor, she clutched onto the radiator, unable to budge for hours, continually pinching herself, self-inflicting pain so as to mitigate the infinite grief that had grasped her heart.

I guess we all wished that this had never happened, but it did, and it changed things forever after. I will never know if men are bad or are simply born liars. Or if they are what Mia accused them all of being that evening, and for the rest of her life.

NEW YORK, 2000 – Angela

My name is Angela and I was born on May 1st, 2000.

How can I best describe the perceptions, movements, and sounds that suddenly became my reality? After much screaming, shouting blood, and shit, I finally discovered their faces – My family, my parents who I had longed to meet. The lights, the crying, the laughter… Sound.

The soft loving sound of their voice whispering love into my tiny ears – Sleeping, crying, and creating my space. I was alive!

On arriving home, my first impression was an awful rattle coming from the subway tracks outside our windows, which was immediately followed by a vibration all around. In time, this unique jolting sensation would become ingrained and would both wake me up in the morning and put me to sleep at night. Strangely enough, I think I would have been thrown off balance had it suddenly disappeared. As days multiplied, so did the sounds, faces, smells, and sensations in general. I kept making all sorts of discoveries. Gifts kept pouring in, many of which I never got to play with. However, my first months of existence were mainly spent lying down or in people's arms – my mother's most of the time. No need to say she adored me.

Marco was around, with a broad, honest smile on his face. He would stare at me in wonder as if pleased to have a sister to look after, but also an accomplice and ally. I guess he felt he was no longer alone when it came to dealing with our parent's ups and downs, their moods, in short, all that happens in a family that one cannot share with strangers, and only a brother or sister fully understand.

Mia was always there for me: I never lacked love in the form of kisses, hugs, or caresses, but deep down I could sense that something was not quite right. I thought that perhaps she was tired or overwhelmed or just simply upset. But instinctively, I soon realized that it had nothing to do with me, that most likely she had a foreboding of what was to come. Some days we would all go out together. It was quite an experience: I was the center of attention, lying like a princess in my pram. On clear days,

I could watch the clouds all puffed up above my face, or the high-rises like needles shooting into the sky. When my parents were in an especially good mood, and they had taken me out on the stroller, they'd attach Jules's to it and I'd be pulled about the streets of Brooklyn as though I were an Eskimo in the North Pole. My dog was not a Husky but it made everyone laugh and happiness floated in and out of the streets.

One day, they insisted that it was time for me to learn how to walk. I hated it at first. I was constantly landing on my poop and, unlike them, I did not find it fun. It really seemed like a useless exercise. Only because they insisted did I persevere and in the end, I managed. My parents were awed and would film my every move, as if I were the product of a miracle. Perhaps I was... It seemed so special to them, and although I felt this huge effort to be of no use, I soon discovered otherwise. In no time was I autonomous; I could go wherever I wanted. No need to wait for things to be given to me or brought. I could fetch them myself.

UPS AND DOWNS

I have many recollections of Mia: drinking her morning coffee, moving hither and thither whilst putting order to the house; crying beside the kitchen table, or smoking one cigarette after another in a state of pure anxiety. At other times, I saw how she smiled with such happiness on seeing Marco coming through the door, and then how she would eclipse herself as soon as she was able to. We were all happy, including Jules, who wouldn't stop wagging his tail. But this happiness was sporadic, as in flashes, when Mia was not crying or arguing with Dad.

Dad too had his ups and downs – I remember how he would call me his precious diamond and hold me in his arms, and I could see his face as it beamed, proud, without a sign of worry in the world. I must say that my parents did not talk much – except, thankfully, when we were all together.

Mia no longer worked her evening jobs. Her only work consisted of going to Meredith's in the mornings. After the niece incident, I was looked after by a middle-aged Polish lady named Olga. She would not only take care of me but also clean and make order in the house. It wasn't much fun, however, between my naps and the walks with Jules, time went by quickly. When Mia returned, in the early afternoon, we would go pick up Marco at school and the fun would begin!

She had begun to frequent the Parson's School studio more often. I believe this was the place in which she felt happiest. Her worries seemed to evanesce while she worked away at her sculptures. She would experiment with all sorts of materials, and the fact that she was surrounded by other budding artists like herself, young, old, white, black, Asian, straight, gay, all sharing their feelings – and sometimes their bodies (Mia was no saint) – was an enormous stimulus for her. She would often take me with her and I'd sit in my stroller watching her hands constantly moving, her fingers molding away until different shapes came into existence. It was fascinating for me and I believe that she seemed at peace with herself in these moments. Her demons were kept at bay and she could get on with what she most liked in the world: creating. Looking back at that brief period of my life with Mia, I can safely say that we were like soulmates. It was as if we were one person. Of course, I was an appendix of hers but there was a secret, silent, communion between us that was extremely powerful and strong. Something magical that I wish could have lasted forever. But then again, I've learned that forever is only a word, in the true world, it does not really exist. Everything comes to end, the good and the bad; pain and pleasure. Nothing lasts. Perhaps in time, only the good memories remain, or so I wish to think.

I also recall that at around this time, Dad would take us for long walks in the park. He would talk to me and my brother about things we hardly understood, but we'd listen in silence for it seemed to us that it was important to him. Sometimes he would cry and this made us terribly sad because we thought it was our fault for no doubt we'd done or said something that had hurt him. I felt awfully sorry for him, but what could I do?

On his thirty-first birthday, Mia organized a huge party to which all the neighbors and a ton of friends showed up. Thanks to her artistic skills, a large collage came to life on our building's façade. It had taken her three days and nights to enlarge the photos of the different body parts that she had taken of the twenty-five tenants who lived within the walls of "The Family" compound. What resulted was an enormous collage, a visual metaphor of all the parts that kept the tenants together as a family. There was loud music, people came in and out, Dad got many presents and I was passed around as if I were "The Family's" mascot. Everyone, it seemed, was having a blast. But even if the party was for Dad, the evening's true protagonist was Marco. Everyone was in awe of him: his manners, his disposition, and his looks. He simply captivated everyone. And I must say that I was not jealous, rather the opposite. I was proud to have such a charming brother and was simply glad to sit there and watch him, when all of a sudden, he fell asleep on the couch next to my stroller.

Unbelievable! Despite the music, the racket, and general noise, he seemed oblivious to it all. Amazing! Like an angel, he was carried away on the wings of Morpheus. Lucky him. At some point during the endless party, I turned around and saw that Mom and Dad were latched onto each other, kissing. It seemed as if they had, for a split moment, reunited, come together, that their differences had all fallen by the wayside, allowing love to pop up its head through the fog of discord. Alas, in hindsight I realize that they were simply shedding the last vestiges of their innocence. And this, in time, would prove to be a painful realization for both of them.

LEUKEMIA

The trees changed color and so did the seasons as if obeying some higher force, and then, one day, I fell sick. I didn't particularly feel sick, but lots of different people around me kept saying so. I heard my parents discuss the fact that I was sick without really understanding what it meant. Our lives changed from one day to the next. Mia and I moved out of the loft into a small room on the other side of the river. It was a very tall building and we were on the eleventh floor, in what was called the Pediatric Ward of the Sloan Kettering Cancer Center. It was full of all kinds of nice people. A bunch of young good-looking nurses and doctors would smile at Mia reassuringly, always making sure that I was well looked after. I remember that the first day I was admitted into this hospital, Mia was in despair, a total wreck.

Nat, a friend from "The Family" compound had accompanied us for what was to be a simple check-up, till the word Leukemia popped out of the doctor's mouth.

"Leukemia."

No sooner had Mia heard the word that she went into some kind of trance, followed by a wailing a hundred times worse than all the screams and tears I had seen her shed in my short-lived life. Although the doctors and nurses were all very kind and nice to me, they nonetheless stuck all sorts of needles into my body. I could feel and then see as my blood would flow through tubes, along with some sort of liquid that was meant to help my body regenerate in some sort of way. It was all very strange, and to tell the truth, rather scary.

What really bothered me, though, was that I was in isolation most of the time and unable to see Marco. Days, weeks, and months went by and Mia, the nurses and I would hang out together. We were becoming a family, a different kind of family than that of the loft, but a family nonetheless. Once in a while, I was allowed to see my friends, who also happened to live in the same ward I was in. Most of us were bald, but we didn't much care. In fact, it strengthened our bond and set us apart in an awkward kind of way. When we were allowed, we would wander around together, each holding onto our medication pole. For some reason, we all seemed to love it and it was in this strange, surreal environment that I really learnt to walk and talk and sing, while I waited for my Dad to come and visit. I always felt Dad's presence, from the very minute he stepped out of the elevator. And at that point nothing else in the world mattered. Although used to the fact, I'd get annoyed and anxious for not being able to run up into what I imagined his outstretched arms.

"Dad! Dad!" I knew he would soon be walking into my room. God, how much I loved my Dad! His eyes filled with tears and happiness to see me; it overwhelmed my little heart... I was such a lucky girl because I knew he loved me just as much as I loved him!

THE FUNERAL

At my funeral, which took place in the Sloan Kettering Garden, lots of people showed up. Meredith and her husband, the nurses, the doctors, friends, family, the hospital priests, rabbis, and even clowns were there... In a strange way it was reminiscent of Mia's parties, except that I was not there; well, what I mean to say is that I was not a guest, and yet I was the main attraction. It's hard to explain.

The day was neither sunny nor cloudy, nor hot or cold. I guess it could be described as a moment captured in time and space, in which pain is so powerful and poignant that none of those present would remember the lofty words or the beautiful music and singing. All that would remain was a bottomless void, loneliness, and emptiness. To think that they had all come together because a sweet, beautiful little girl had passed away and they would never see her again, was beyond anyone's comprehension.

It was unthinkable to believe that one day I would die; die before my time and leave them bereft, alone, and suffering.

Mia was in her finest, all dressed up for the occasion with the solemnity that the occasion required. She wore a black hat, heels, and a black silk skirt. The idea that she somehow looked like a Sicilian widow, seeing her Don to the grave, helped in that she was able to get through the ceremony without breaking down. She was so brave, and I was so, so proud of her. How much I would have liked to tell her so. I know she felt as though she could not let me down, and I must say she did not. Oh, how much I loved her. The scene from the above was that of a sorrowful garden, where grief, despair, impotence, anger, and so many other expressions of pain were made manifest. If God were a witness, I am sure that He too must have shed tears. I remember seeing the gynecologist who brought me into the world, crying, clutching onto to his assistant's knee; Livia, who had flown in from Italy the day before, was holding onto Mia's hand so tightly that both their hands became numb, and Nat with her husband Zack were desperately trying to comfort Dad, who was absolutely destroyed. The Witches came across like hieratic statues, silently holding onto Marco's hand, and resembled the chorus in some ancient Greek tragedy. It was very sad, but also beautiful and moving, for it was out of love for me and my family that everyone had gathered. Dad and Mia, who sat together, never once turned to each or even let their bodies graze. My loss had turned what was a gap into a mighty chasm, where a waterfall of tears came crashing down in between them. As I could have foretold, this would after keep them apart forever.

The ceremony was officiated by an American African reverend whom we had met at the hospital. He had become a good friend of Mia's and had done his very best to make sense of all that had happened. As if finding a sense could somehow make things better or mitigate the pain...

Only Mia and Dad's parents were missing, but that is yet another story which may be told one day.

PART III

NEW YORK CITY, 2005 – Lizbeth Orlinsky

As she walked into The Gramercy Tavern, Mia's long-time waitressing friend, Devon, an openly gay, typical New Yorker, was there to greet her:

"Welcome Bitch! How are you darling? Looking good sister, looking good..."

"Ha! Devon, you're the one who's looking fabulous, as always."

"*Le PD* is waiting for you. Watch out, sister, make sure you get what you deserve..."

Louis, as was customary, was sitting at his favorite table, looking like a clean and perfect version of the Queen of Queens, with stretched-out arms, ready to hug her:

"Champagne? *Ma Superstar?*"

As she neared, she noticed that he was impeccably dressed as was his wont, but his blood-shot eyes and the white foam on the corners of his mouth confirmed that he was in full "Louis mode".

"How about a strong Bloody Mary, *mon cher Louis?*"

Mia figured everything must have been sold, but with Louis, everything was never enough. She wondered who on earth was the perfectly made-up doll, sitting at his table. After a brief introduction and a few words about whether they had friends in common, the doll planted a kiss on Mia's cheek. Her name was Lizbeth, and Louis was convinced that all three would have lots to gain if they agreed on some sort of collaboration.

'Merde!' thought Mia: this was supposed to be a simple celebration between Louis and her, and she had no energy for this.

Lizbeth Orlinsky was born in Washington, D.C., where her father worked as some sort of consultant or lobbyist for the White House. She was in her late thirties and had graduated from Columbia University with honors. Additionally, and which was what Louis liked most about her, she was married to Oleg – an extremely wealthy real-estate New York entrepreneur of Russian extraction. As Mia took in all this biographical information about Lizbeth, she wondered why people made such an effort to promote themselves, one way or another. Why? What was the reason behind this strong urge? Did it really matter, deep down, and what was there to gain? She had no answer to this mystery. On the other hand, Louis couldn't care less if Lizbeth was talented or not, or how well, if at all, she and Mia would get along. All he cared about was his access to Oleg's filthy rich circle of connections and friends who would bring his gallery and his income to the next level. Moreover, making his way into the Washington political elite was not something to be missed.

Despite the three Bloody Mary Mia had pounded down, she clearly understood what Louis was suggesting, or rather, imposing. And a few, never-ending hours later, tired, drunk and bored, Mia could take no more chit-chat. She invited them both to her favorite happy hour joint, hoping they would decline. Louis was too precious and most certainly had "better things to do", but Lizbeth, surprisingly, accepted. Again, in his clean and perfect version of the Queen of Queens, Louis said:

"You ladies have given me all the excitement I needed for one day! I'll head home. Lizbeth, please give my regards to Oleg and don't be late, we all know how worried he gets for you. And Mia, *please* behave, you know exactly what I mean, don't you?"

Mia was quite used to his patronizing tone and didn't pay much attention to it anymore, but she was now certain that Louis's proposal of working with Lizbeth was something she could not refuse. She had signed a two-year exclusivity agreement with his gallery, and if she were ever to breach this agreement, she would be the bigger loser of the two.

Half an hour later, as they entered Kastro's in the lower east side, Mia felt at home. The cobwebs and the fishy clientele, most of whom were playing backgammon, greeted her. It didn't take long for Mia to recognize familiar faces and she headed straight towards them.

"Mia, baby, helllooooooooo!"

"Oh my God, so good to see you! Hello, boys!" Kisses and hugs and more kisses were rapidly exchanged.

"Can we have a quick strong one?"

"Of course, come and sit with us! So how are you? Your show went really well, didn't it?" said one.

"Congratulations, superstar!" said another.

Huh? Superstar? That was some accolade. Did she really look like she was wearing a crown and a cape of some sort? As far as I was concerned, it looked more like a hair clip and a *pashmina*... no matter.

"I just finished lunch with Louis, he never stops, does he?" Her tone was affectionate, and she had all but forgotten about Lizbeth, whom she now realized had disappeared. She stood up to look for her; besides she needed to pee. When Mia found Lizbeth, she was sitting at a table with an interesting-looking man who must have been in his fifties. He had an open laptop beside him and, gathering from the bags under his eyes, it looked as if he might have been writing for quite a while.

She walked up to them, and as she went to introduce herself (which seemed the correct thing to do), she missed the low stool that was right in front of them, and tripped over it, landing directly into the man's crotch, along with all the drinks that were on their table. And even though the entire scene must have not taken more than a few seconds, the commotion it caused was quite dreadful. Lizbeth jumped up out of her velvet armchair, with horror, as if she were witnessing a multiple murder. And the distinguished-looking man was almost knocked over along with his computer by Mia who was all over him, screaming at the top of her voice, *"Fuck! Puttana Eva! Merde!"* For a split second, their bodies, felt wonderful together.

"Oh My God, Oh My God, I am so, so sorry," said Mia, apologizing effusively, all while trying to get up and detach her body from his.

"Mia! What are you doing?" screamed Lizbeth, absolutely embarrassed.

"I am sorry, I was looking for you, and thought you'd left."

"No, I am still here, as you can see. Now I understand what Louis meant when he said you should behave. Damn it!"

'What a filthy little bitch!' Mia thought to herself.

"Yes, I guess Louis is always right," she hissed.

"At least nobody got hurt. Are you okay, Mia? And you, Patrick?"

"Oh, me? Yes, yes, of course. I am okay, thank you. I am Patrick, by the way," he said, as he tried to dry off his computer.

Mia smiled. "I am happy to meet you, Patrick, and again, please accept my most sincere apologies," she said, with a forced smile as Lizbeth looked on.

Embarrassed and confused, Mia felt that she had made a fool of herself. Her legendary clumsiness was no secret, but this time around, all the alcohol that she had ingested throughout the day had not helped. As she walked away, one of her high heels began to make a strange sound, a kind of clink-clonk, which accompanied her as she headed for the exit and all the way home.

It had been a long and tiresome day: the walk to school, meeting Hermès, the never-ending lunch... It was now time to pick Marco up at school and she was, as usual, going to be late.

When she got there, Marco greeted her with his customary broad smile. Hand in hand, they walked back home – he didn't give a damn if she was barefoot, her broken heals in her bag. A TV pizza dinner was in order, and afterward, Mia watched as my big brother fell asleep in her comfortable bed. She loved him so much; her little big-eyed forest *gnometto*. Although she was happy to have Marco by her side, these were also the moments in which Mia felt loneliest. Alone, with the weight of the world on her shoulders, in a city that was not and never would be hers to claim. She missed her family, her hills, Livia, The Witches, and her beloved Jonas.

Jonas! I now realize I haven't mentioned him yet: my godfather, the most cheerful, kindest person on the planet after Marco! He and Mia were born on the exact same day, January 10th, 1973. Jonas's mother was Finnish and grandma's best friend. They had grown up practically as siblings, like twins always longing to be together, even when they were in different countries.

Jonas had tried the New York life for a few years, going to NYU film school, but in the end left the city, heartbroken after my passing. It was the final straw, and he found New York to be too tough a place. His move to Ibiza had been quick. There, he could write his film scripts in peace and quiet.

Most of all Mia missed me, Dad, and a life that seemed to have slipped through her fingers, like sand. A life she had wished for so hard and was now gone. She hesitated to call Dad, but knew better, and having learnt the hard way, was not about to risk one of his outbursts of anger and bitterness. This was not something she could handle tonight. She poured herself one last glass of white wine, rolled herself a spliff and called Jonas. It was 10 p.m. and perhaps he might care to accompany her with a glass of wine on his side of the world.

SPAGHETTI *AGLIO, OLIO E PEPERONCINO*

The rest of the week was relatively smooth. Mia had decided that she would not answer any calls, except those coming from Meredith – who checked in on her regularly – and from Livia, who kept her updated on the earthquake aftermath. For his part, Louis had left a series of messages to discuss the collaboration with Lizbeth, as if she had already agreed to it. Everything felt numb, till Dad called, proposing that she and Marco join him for dinner on Saturday; Mia accepted happily, hoping they would behave like adults. It had been a long time since the three of them had been together. Boy, did she miss him/them...

When they arrived at Dad's apartment on Saturday evening, Mia immediately felt that things were going to get nasty as Dad was completely drunk. He had invited them for a *spaghetti aglio, olio e pepperoncino* dinner, but as they arrived, they found the spaghetti all over the floor and the *peperoncino* had made it into Dad's eyes, which were all red and wet.

As Dad pathetically tried to grab Mia, telling her all sorts of things, Marco quietly picked up the spaghetti from the floor. It took a while for Dad to somewhat sober up and for Mia to fix a quick dinner while trying to ignore his horrible mumblings and the atrocious allegations he was heaping on her. All of a sudden, Dad stepped over the line and accused Mia of being responsible for my death.

Silent evil shouts in the night...
'Oh... no...! Please, Mia, no!'

Had she only turned around then and there and left; or thought it through, but no. There was no time for thinking. Her blood rushed to her temples like lava rising to the surface of a volcano, and she rushed to the cutlery cabinet, pulled out a knife, and pointed it straight at Dad – Marco quickly crept under the table.

You must believe me, dear reader, when I tell you that I invoked all the powers in the universe to stop her. By now the knife was right under my father's chin, grazing his neck. And then, darkness descended on this horrifying scene.

All the lights in the apartment went off. Had I managed a little miracle?

A few seconds later, the lights came back on, and Marco, like the hero that he is, although crying and scared, crept out from beneath the table, went up to Mia, and slowly took the knife from her hand. It could have been the scene from some scary movie, but it was no movie; it was my family and Marco was saving the day. I will forever be grateful to him for his bravery, but above all, his love.

Dad ran to his room.

Silent evil shouts in the night...

Mia and Marco hugged each other with all their might, both scared and relieved. Sobbing, Marco finally fell asleep on the couch and Mia was so riddled with guilt and shame that she was unable to either sleep or go home. What a disaster. If there is a lesson to take away from this dreadful episode, it is that one should never go back when there is nothing left.

When Marco was finally asleep, Mia crept up to Dad's door and knocked softly. No answer. She was still in time to turn back, to call it a night, but no, she wasn't getting a no for an answer, so she turned the door's handle, walked straight into room and into Dad's bed, who at first stirred like an innocent victim. They smelt each other, like two animals before mating and in a split second were totally naked. They stared into each other's eyes, just like they had done in their previous life, waiting to see what came next. He held his gaze, with a sweet, innocent expression, while she just stared into his face, both knowing full well that they had long left each other's shore and there was no chance of reconciliation. For the next couple of hours, however, they made love as if it were their first – and last – time.

All the saints and spirits of the universe which I had invoked, in the end deserted me. It was clear that they might accept a pink sky or two and a few cool helping tricks, but they were certainly not going to abide by this kind of crazy behavior.

The sun had just risen when Mia slipped out of bed and grabbed her clothes lying on the floor. She hardly knew what to do. Should she grab breakfast for the three of them or head back to her place like a fugitive on the run? Or simply pretend that nothing had happened and wake Dad and Marco up? It was Sunday, and once upon a time, on Sundays, they would all go for brunch. Those moments now seemed like something so far in the past that they even came across as absurd.

As she crept quietly out of the room, she saw black and white pictures of Meredith's works hanging along the corridor. Some of the cast-iron installations in the making, others of the studio, others of the day of their inauguration in Central Park – so many distant memories – Dad was clearly living in the past.

She decided to head back to her place, with a million conflicting thoughts running through her head, like falling stars crisscrossing the firmament when all of a sudden she changed her mind and decided to trust the gods (whatever that meant) and head to the nearest Deli to grab a few cream cheese bagels with salmon on the side and chocolate doughnuts to take back to Dad and Marco.

It was Sunday after all, and she was going to try to make the best out of the moment.

As she returned from the Deli, she found the door to Dad's apartment unlocked, just as she had left it. Marco was still fast asleep, and without making a sound, she dropped the paper bags on the kitchen table, undressed, and slipped back into bed, where Dad was lying in the same exact position that she'd left him in. She brought her body next to his, hoping, in her subconscious, that she'd experience the same feeling she had when they first lied in each other's arms. But no, it was no longer the same man, neither one of them were the same persons. She closed her eyes and thankfully fell back to sleep.

All three woke up more or less at the same time. When Marco realized that his parents had slept in the same bed, he pretended it was no big deal and behaved as though it were nothing special. Secretly, however, he was happy no blood had been shed and hoped Mia would get the hell out of there before things would turn awry once more. Mia made coffee with the *Bialetti* and in no time the apartment filled up with the aroma of the good old days. For a minute it felt like they were a real family. They had breakfast without saying much to one another, but at least they managed to be together, and it was a semblance of normality, of sanity. When they finished breakfast, Mia left them to their Sunday football-related activities, and headed home – alone, "a*vec la queue entre les jambes"*, dreading the thought of emptiness that awaited her.

A terrible feeling of loss and failure hung above her head, and she felt absolutely despondent. It would have been the perfect time for Hermès to make one of his apparitions and take her on one of their boozy brunches, but it wouldn't be so this time around.

With her beloved friends being on the other side of the world and feeling slightly lonely she decided to do something completely unexpected: she called Lizbeth and invited her out for brunch at The Odeon. This would be her own way of trying to be responsible, please Louis and maybe, if the situation was favorable, ask about Patrick.

As luck would have it, Lizbeth was not available for brunch, but before Mia had time to even think about her "luck", Lizbeth invited her over for dinner that same night at her home! Although Mia was never very good with dinner invitations on Sunday evenings, she accepted. Hopefully, she would not mess it up.

PART IV

NEW YORK, 2005 – Sunday dinner at the Olinskys

After having spent the Sunday afternoon watching dumb TV shows and having a few glasses of wine, it was finally time to get ready. She had fought the temptation of finding excuses not to go to what she imagined would be a very tedious dinner party.

She opened her closet, hoping to find the "miraculous" outfit: the one that would show her in her best light. Did she not have to pretend and live up to other people's expectations? It was always the same: one had to play the part, to anticipate what others thought instead of being oneself. The most annoying thing was that in the end, she was no longer sure who she was herself. What the hell was she going to wear? There had to be a solution to her dilemma somewhere inside her closet. Six different outfits were tried on and discarded; nothing seemed to work. Finally, her eye fell on the old, but faithful, black cocktail dress. It had long sleeves, which would cover her arms, where a worn out "I love you so much" tattoo showed – it looked more like some weird balloon with Egyptian hieroglyphics that no longer made any sense.

The dress was tight, but not so tight as to hide her beer belly, and with her high heels, she was confident that her legs – which she still doted on – would keep any gawker's eyes away from all the rest. She finally found her lipstick at the bottom of her bag, which not only would bring her sallow lips back to life, but also give color to her cheeks. She then applied a double coat of mascara and thankfully, found her favorite hair clip. Lastly, she retrieved her most precious belonging out of its hiding place: The *Anish Kapoor* good luck ring. And with two spare pairs of black tights in her bag – for once – she was ready to head out on time and looking good!

The Olinskys lived on Central Park West. *Ghost Busters* had been filmed in their building in the early 80's, and Mia felt that if she had the gumption to go all the way there, she could pretty much go anywhere. Feeling lady-like, she chose to call a cab instead of taking the subway. For once, she felt pretty damn good with herself and took a deep breath, filling her lungs with a reassuring air – Louis was going to have to reimburse her for this cab ride, that's for sure!

When the taxi finally arrived at her destination, she walked up to the doorman, who accompanied her to the keyed elevator and entered the Penthouse's code. All of a sudden, she got cramps. What had gotten into her? Where was the self-confidence, she was exuding a minute ago?

Too late. It was way too late to change her mind or turn on her heels.

Ting!

The elevator doors had opened, all while an Asian butler in white gloves gently bowed to greet her, while asking if he could take her coat. He then led her towards the living room, a model-like waitress was standing with a tray of glasses in her hand. She was about to grab a glass, when out of the blue Lizbeth appeared, throwing her arms around Mia's neck, as if they were best of friends. Having lived in N.Y. for a few years, Mia was accustomed, and at times even enjoyed the superficiality with which people acted with one another, but this was rather weird. Was "little miss perfect" already drunk or on drugs?

"Mia! Darling! I'm so, so happy you could make it! It's wonderful to have you with us. Oleg! Oleg! Come, come… everyone: this is Mia, the sculptor I told you all about, and my future partner!"

Everyone turned around, and Oleg slouched towards her like a leopard sizing his prey. He was completely bald but quite fit, and clearly very proud of himself. He greeted her somewhere between a nod and a full bow, staring at her with grey icy eyes. Where on earth had she landed? She felt as if all the other guests were looking at her, and as she looked back all that crossed her mind was whether her tights were in place or if they had fallen to her knees. She took a deep breath, brought her stomach in, and said to herself: *'Come on Mia! You can do this! Breathe in, breathe out!'*

"*Je suis enchantée,* Oleg. Thank you for this most unexpected and wonderful invitation." Why was she speaking French to this Russian fellow?

"I've heard marvelous things about you, and I am delighted that you will be working with Lizbeth on her new project," Oleg said, with a thick Russian accent.

Project? Hers? Whatever… Louis would have some explaining to do tomorrow.

"Please, come, Mia, make yourself at home. Let me introduce you to some of our best friends," Oleg, went on, as he slipped his hand down her back onto her ass. As discretely as possible, she brushed his hand off her behind, resisting the temptation of whacking him, and instead opting to play the part, even if only for this one night.

"This is Olga, my sister and her boyfriend Mäns von den Bruck, and this is Tatiana Ustinov and her husband,

John Henry Graham, and last but not least, Contessa Smeralda Suguccio, with whom you can speak Italian, and her husband Patrick Cenovis, whom you have already met, I believe." Lizbeth, who was standing beside her husband, gave her a knowing look. *'Cenovis?'* Mia almost burst out laughing.

Cenovis is a Swiss vegetable paste that nobody else in the world seems to like except for Mia, Livia, Jonas, and myself. This must be a sign, Mia thought to herself. She displayed her enchanted smile, proving to herself that she should have become an actress instead of fabricating things that deep down no one really understood.

She might have actually enjoyed this whole *mise-en-scène* if she hadn't had to constantly hold her breath to make sure her stomach didn't stick out. Her eyes kept searching desperately for the waitress with the champagne tray, which she now spotted at the other end of the room. But she couldn't very well leap across the room to grab a glass. It was only when Lizbeth left her alone to go to the kitchen that Mia, like a cat on a mission, stealthily made her way towards the champagne. She finally got a hold of the long-sought glass of sparkling golden bubbles which she downed in one gulp, quickly grabbing another, trusting no one, except the waitress, had noticed her avidity. As she wet her lips on her second tulip-like cup, Mia was able to take a better look around.

The apartment, though fancy, was tacky but the views over Central Park and Manhattan were stunning! She figured Oleg was a Russian fellow, who like so many of his countrymen, had made a lot of money after the fall of the Soviet Union. Everyone seemed very much at ease with one another, and she soon realized that she was the only who had come unaccompanied.

The rest of the women looked stunning, in their designer-label clothes and bedecked with their expensive jewelry, chatting away with one another about their summer residences in The Hamptons and how well their children were doing in their different, upscale, private schools.

Trying to pass unnoticed, Mia made her way to a bookshelf. As she examined the book's spines for their titles, she remembered having once read a quote by Jay McInerney: "In the examination of personal libraries lies the basis of character analysis." Unfortunately, the present selection was a rather poor one, and Mia figured that she would have to take a different approach to figure out who Lizbeth really was. As she was about to turn away from the minimalistic bookshelves that rose up to the ceiling, she suddenly felt someone's presence behind her, and then a man's voice:

"Do you like reading?"

She could practically feel his breath on her neck. It was Mr. Cenovis.

'*Cristo Santo della Madonna!*' She thought to herself. He was so bloody sexy that she almost lost her footing and found herself holding onto the minimalistic bookshelf, which thankfully was sturdy even if it did not contain too many volumes on its shelves.

"Yes, I do, especially minds," she answered in the corniest way possible.

"So, aside from falling on top of strangers and making wonderful art, you can also read minds? In that case, I'd better stay away…" he added.

Mia laughed out loud, too loud! The room turned towards them and she blushed as red as a tomato. Everyone, especially Smeralda, looked at her suspiciously. After that, Lizbeth thankfully came back announcing that dinner was ready and that it would be served in the dining room.

"*Diner assis-placé,*" Lizbeth added, with a smile.

'Come on Mia, you can do this. Breathe in, breathe out; and make sure to hold your stomach in!'

Since they were nine, Mia was placed at the head of the table with Patrick and Lizbeth on her right and left sides respectively. It was a tradition at the Olinskys' to start every meal with a shot of vodka; a shot that was repeated in-between each serving. The evening was actually turning out to be a much easier affair than she initially envisaged. The conversations were, for the most part, rather superficial and as hours rolled by, they became louder and louder. It was clear that this bunch of so-called art lovers had fallen for Mia. They had clearly followed Louis and Lizbeth's advice and bought her work on her show's opening night. And Mia knew exactly how to play them. To put on the detached, artsy personae, which would captivate them. Patrick spoke of his job as *Le Figaro's* U.S. stinger, while Lizbeth seemed over the moon about her project with Mia. Accustomed to handling strong liquor, Mia kept up with the conversation better than the rest and when allowed to remove her high-heals, she could manage the situation as if she owned it. After the second Bison Vodka sorbet had been served, the guests began taking turns to go to the bathroom to "powder" themselves, either alone or accompanied, making everyone increasingly talkative and all-powerful. In any case, this seemed to be the source of the party's fuel. In her skimpy red-silk, Chinese-like dress, Lizbeth, who had also taken her shoes off, at one point rushed out of her dressing room, holding a cucumber as though it were a microphone. *'What on earth did this dildo-like vegetable have anything to do with the situation?* Mia thought.

"I know you think I'm a dumbbell, but when I see you, Mia, I imagine you naked, working on your next sculpture, and me with my camera filming, I'm sure I'll be able to capture your true essence and be able to show the world your true nature," she shrieked.

Filming Mia's true "naked" nature could easily turn out to be a horror movie, but at this point, Mia was having enough fun to smile and nod as if in agreement. Soon thereafter, Lizbeth and Oleg disappeared into their room and Smeralda decided it was time to join her husband and Mia on the balcony. Olga and Tatiana followed, while their respective husbands went into the studio to, most probably, "powder up".

"Let's have a last cigarette," Patrick suggested, clearly annoyed by the new arrivals.

'Mia, go home, go home,' a voice spoke inside her head.

I want to believe that she somehow heard my voice and without a word, blew a kiss to all, quickly slipped back into her shoes, and finding her way out, even managing to thank the butler and the model-like waitress – who seemed rather used to all this *fracas* – made her way to the elevator. It took a while for her to find a cab on Central Park West, which seemed strange to Mia. It was 2.00 a.m. on a Sunday night and no doubt every neighborhood had its own peculiar schedules. When she finally did find a cab, she dozed off in the back seat and the driver had to wake her up upon arrival. Finally, home! The night had been much more fun than she expected, which pleased her, especially since there had been no damage; *no faux pas...*

It felt good. She quickly undressed and put on her favorite and most comfortable T-shirt and pulled out her weed box, all while opening her room's window. She just lay there, on her bed, smoking her well-deserved spliff. Pure bliss.

Marco was with his father this week, and for a moment she felt as if she had no worries in the world. She did not have to get up the next morning and could relax. The vodka was running through her veins and after taking a few hits she felt as she was floating in space, comfortably dozing off in the clean smell of her white sheets. Suddenly, the buzzer rang but given her close-to-comatose state, she ignored it. It kept buzzing and buzzing, shattering her well-being. Unable to stand the stridden noise, she pulled herself out of bed and went to the interphone and hollered:

"Who the hell is it?"

"It's me, Patrick, let me in now or I'll knock your door down," was yelled back at her.

Mia buzzed him in, and as she opened the door, she could hear him running up the stairs. In two seconds, he was in her loft looking like he had just run a marathon. There was nothing to say, nothing to do. Their mouths immediately met and they crashed on the floor not even able to reach the bed. Like a perfect puzzle, by 6 a.m. they were whispering their love for each other, deliriously mixing sex and affection.

Holy mother of God, what a weekend.

NAKED BODY, NAKED SOUL

It so happened that although Smeralda (alias Mrs. Cenovis) was deliriously jealous of the situation, she had been the one who had proposed a free and open relationship with Patrick in the first place. Her non-stop flings over the years with all sorts of women and men had not been easy for Patrick to accept, but he had gone along with it and now, it seemed it was her turn to endure the burden of her choices. Mia knew that sooner or later, Smeralda would strike back, and she wasn't sure she was ready for the drama, but two weeks into the relationship – albeit Mia's efforts to be as discreet as possible – this was turning out to be an intense affair, both physically and emotionally. In Patrick, Mia had discovered a tenderness that she had all but forgotten, and Patrick rediscovered what having sex was all about (and also discovered Brooklyn) – for better or for worse!

As they were having a late lunch at the *Broadway Diner* and Patrick's hand was caressing Mia's leg under her skirt, she wondered what he really meant to her. His hand felt wonderful as it neared her crotch, so much so, that she closed her eyes with pleasure. In no time he would be grabbing a cab to go back to the office, and she would be off to pick Marco up at school.

These days Mia's mind was constantly absorbed by Patrick, which explains why she was as absentminded as she was during her meetings with Louis and Lizbeth when the details of the performance were being finalized. She figured that her physical presence would conceal her total lack of interest, which is why she had only vaguely realized that she was going to be the star of a "sculpt-live performance" in an empty garage in the Meat Packing District.

Mia couldn't care less and had no interest whatsoever in listening to the never-ending details of the event. As happens with all liaisons, especially in their infancy, she was infatuated and all she could think about was her new lover and their passionate encounters. So, she kept saying yes to everything and paying no attention to what she was signing, let alone agreeing to. The night of the Performance rolled around in the blink of an eye.

The show was planned in ten days and would last one night (from 9 p.m. to 3 a.m.). It was going to be filmed by Lizbeth and aired live on a private Russian TV Channel. The bidding to acquire the piece would be managed directly by Louis's gallery.

It was a late September afternoon, and a soft but balmy breeze caressed the City. Mia arrived in the empty garage early afternoon where the set-up was practically finalized; video technicians were working on the last details of the camera installations and a three-meter chunk of fresh clay was wrapped in plastic and vertical sprinklers installed so that it wouldn't dry.

As soon as he saw her, Louis ran up to her.

"*Ma* Superstar, my Darling! Here you are! Isn't it just unbelievable? I already have the P.A.'s of our Russian oligarchs pestering me on my cellphone. They can't wait for the auction to start! Are you ready?"

Mia was speechless; what she was about to do had only recently begun to creep up on her. She had not slept a wink the previous night and had not even dared confide in Livia. She had told Jonas and The Witches and although the latter were open to almost anything, they hated Mia getting into this public, commercial wannabe artist thing.

"Mia Darling, look: a hundred chairs for our guests go here, the bar there, the catering space is on the left, and your dressing room with fridge, table and all that you need is ready."

"Louis, do I really have to do this?"

"Mia! We've freaking been talking about it for weeks, don't you dare pull back and make a fool out of me. You're going to perform and there is nothing else to say, you spoiled bitch!"

"Fuck you, Louis!"

"I don't care how the fuck you're going to do it, but you're doing it! *Tu m'as compris, n'est ce pas?*"

The tone of his voice had changed. It somehow reminded Mia of her father. His eyes were bloodshot, his lips were as tight as a knife blade, and he seemed determined not to let her get away with this last-minute hesitancy. The show was going to start in a few hours and she was at a total loss. Her mind went blank.

As she exited the garage, she started walking, not knowing where to go. Her first thought – as soon as she felt the balmy breeze caress her face – was for Marco, whose Maman was about to perform naked in front of a hundred guests and the Russian elite. Thank God, Dad had told her that he had no intention of witnessing this so-called art performance. Dad. Dad who once more had vanished from Mia's life just as she had tried to erase their last evening together from her memory. And what about Patrick? Where was he now when she needed him most? Patrick who had obsessed and distracted her from all of this, he too had vanished. Mia tried reaching him several times while on her way back home, but he did not pick up the phone. He had, however, promised to attend the Performance.

Was he just one more phony in a series that had come in and out of Mia's life? When she reached her place, she finally went straight to bed and laid there, trying to gather her thoughts, too nervous to move beyond the safety of her room. She didn't even dare have a drink or a smoke. She just lay there, petrified, letting the hours roll by, hoping that another day would dawn, and this nightmare become something of the past.

But it wouldn't be so: Louis, who in the meantime had left numerous messages on her cell, finally decided to come and pick her up at her place.

"Mia, Mia," she heard him yelling from the street below her window.

She looked out, and there he was, standing in front of a limousine, in a gray Tom Ford suit, holding an enormous bouquet of red roses. Mia could not but smile at his perseverance. She grabbed her things, locked the door behind her, got into the car, and switched to battle mode. In the worst-case scenario, Mia thought, foolishly, she would just skip town once the show was over.

"*Je suis désolé, mon amour*, I don't know what got into me for speaking to you like that, please forgive me. I do not recognize myself; this town makes us all crazy," purred Louis.

Mia didn't say a word. She understood Louis's true nature well enough, his ambition and greed; however, she also had to admit that she was no victim, either. Neither his nor anyone else's. It was her responsibility and, who knows? If she survived, this just might be the turning point in her languishing career. Had she not wanted to be an actress, too, at some point? The answer was clearly yes, but not exactly a porn one... *'Oh, well,'* she thought: life is just one big performance, at times tragic and at others comic – but a performance nonetheless.

Once they reached the garage, the limousine pulled up onto the red carpet and Lizbeth ran up to them wearing a long red dress. Cameras were already rolling and the adrenaline started to rise from Mia's guts straight to her heart and head. Curious neighbors and anonymous New Yorkers had slowly gathered around the perimeter. Two bodyguards stood at the entrance, making sure all ran smoothly, while two hostesses carefully checked the names on their rosters of the guests who filed past. Mia needed no checking. Everyone knew she was the star – or buffoon – of the night's entertainment. With Lizbeth holding her hand and Louis walking behind them, Mia made her way to the "stage" for her first performance. Tonight, at least, she wouldn't have to worry about her tights... After her initial unease and diffidence, she dropped her coat and the performance got underway. Accompanied by live musicians and DJs, she started molding pieces of clay and plaster on a steel rod – naked.

From the outside, it looked like she was having the time of her life. The spectators loved every minute of it. The so-called art collectors went wild with the sexual-techno aspect of the performance.

Her "tree of life" sculpture ended up selling for just over $300.000 – which was an absolute record amount for an emerging artist like herself. Louis practically fainted when he heard the final price, and Lizbeth was overjoyed and proud of "her" performance.

A NIGHT TO BE REMEMBERED

Patrick had shown up with his wife Smeralda. When they came within earshot distance, she looked Mia straight in the eye, and blurted out laughing:

"I would like to wish you *in bocca al lupo*," she said, "but in your case I best wish you, *in culo alla balena*!"

Afterwards, and during the whole performance, Patrick had the gall of kissing Smeralda, and holding hands with her throughout the entire evening as if they were madly in love or had recently met. Mia's passion, or whatever it was or she wanted to call it, ended that night, as swiftly as it had begun. *'What a fucking douchebag!'* One more man into Mia's bag of liars...

The months that followed the performance had a strong impact on Mia's life. She had finally received her much sought-after recognition; unfortunately, though, it did not make her feel any less lonely or empty. Quite the opposite: the magic potion had now become a regular treat, and a necessary one in order to face all the people she had come into contact with but didn't really care for *(vice-versa)*. And, actually, let us face it: Why not admit it? When Marco was with Dad, she partied her nights away most of the time playing backgammon at *Kastro's*.

Unlike Dad, Meredith relished Mia's success; she felt it was thanks to her that Mia had made it in New York. She would let everyone and their mother (and their mother's mother!) know – whenever the chance arose – that Mia had been her protégé and that, had it not been for her, she would still be toiling away in obscurity.

Nonno, as was expected, found the whole affair disturbing and demeaning and refrained from ever calling Mia about it or anything else for that matter. Mia had finally come to the realization that some people never change. Their personalities – whether good or bad – are only accentuated with time. They grow like noses and ears.

Mr. Cenovis, on the other hand, had tried to contact Mia on numerous occasions after the performance. Unfortunately for him, this time around, she had closed all doors, both physical and figuratively speaking. Besides, she had heard from Lizbeth that Smeralda was expecting a child, and she sure was not going to be anybody's "niece".

As for Dad, he had played the "niece's card", not once but many times, and in the end, he was as lonely as a dog. His bad habits had gotten out of control altogether. It was impossible to tell if he were simply jealous of Mia's success or of the fact that she had been able to keep the demons at bay and stay clear of that dark side with its ugly old remorse. In the end, Meredith agreed that it would be best for Dad to go back to Umbria, with good old Jules, and manage her studio there, which he did.

Mia and Marco were left alone in New York.

ZERO

At some point, a few months after the performance, Mia slowly but surely lost all notion of time, space, place, and most importantly, purpose. She no longer seemed to care about anything or anyone. The only thing that existed was herself, and quite often, she even had difficulty figuring out who on earth she was. In short, she was gone.

Every single need, responsibility, or care had been put aside. She simply shut down. Her life had become an egotistical rollercoaster, and any feeling or respect that she might have had for those around her seemed to have disappeared altogether. The never-ending nights, fueled by all sorts of substances, had become a routine. Night and day had become one big haze, and her work, her child, and her responsibilities had been flung out the window. She ignored reality and tried, as best she could, to convince herself and everyone around her that there was nothing left for her to fight for – in short, to keep on living.

Marco had never felt as lonely: first, he had lost me, then Dad and Jules took off, and all he was left with was Mia's physical presence, which was far from enough, since her behavior, was, like I said, totally messed up. However, in spite of all the challenges, the ups and downs, the madness and instability, he never ceased being the indigo kid he had always been, with a heart of gold and the kindness of a prince.

But somehow, maybe miraculously, having reached ground zero and there being nowhere deeper to sink, Mia realized that either she had to throw in the towel for good, or she had to fight the battle of her life; to save herself, Marco, and my memory. And this is exactly what she did – she defeated the demons once and for all, struggled to come back up to the surface and breathe again.

For zero is not only rock bottom, but also the point from which one can turn back and swim towards the light. The light of hope and happiness. Once more the metaphor of water seemed to permeate her thoughts: she needed the sea, the rivers, the rain… All that water represented for her came back in a flood. She needed the cleansing power of water – in all its manifestations.

So, she started swimming and swam and swam and swam.

PART V

ST. LUC, 2020

Some kind of crazy virus, which towards the end of 2019 had spread from central China to the rest of the world, and was killing thousands, had brought the world to its knees and forced people around the globe to confine themselves in their homes, for fear the pandemic would, like a brush fire, destroy all of humankind. This had brought about all sorts of additional problems: the elderly were dying in the solitude of their homes or in nursing homes, the young could hardly comprehend what the matter was, and in those families in which strife already existed, it took on a more sinister and dangerous turn. Thankfully, nature had been given a respite: no planes, no cars, no pollution, and the sea and sky and all its habitat were thankful for this most needed time off from the constant soiling of the planet.

Lots had happened to Mia in these fifteen intervening years. She had left N.Y. and a life which had become absolutely superficial and, moreover, dangerous. Mia realized that she left dear friends behind, but it had become a matter of survival, and she could no longer cope with the asphalt jungle. She needed a return to the roots, to her native soil, to her rolling Umbrian hills, where her olive groves and unlabeled wines, and real fare could still be had.

By no means had it been an easy ride. She still had her good and bad days. On this particular one, she was in the middle of one of her mood swings and was puttering around the garden, trying to make herself useful.

Birds were chirping like mad, and it seemed to her that their singing had never been as loud and clear as on that spring morning.

At the rear of the garden, overlooking the woods and the little river, there was a sign which read: *LE pAsaGe seKret*, written by a child's hand. If one were to follow the trail, which was flanked on either side by thread handrails, one would reach a few simple little tree houses which had been built with sticks and stones scattered next to the riverbed.

That afternoon, two kids were playing beside the huts, laughing and discussing the latest Naruto episode and such things as *toupies beyblades...*

One was blond, with a beaming, white-skinned face and a toothless mouth; the other looked exactly like a boy version of me. It was mind-boggling, and I marveled to behold the power of nature. It filled me with such joy that I thought it was nothing short of a miracle. I was in awe.

GIULIO AND LEON!

They were my little brothers. Brothers with whom I had never had the chance of interacting, but my brothers all the same. They knew of my existence and often spoke about me.

It was April 15th, Livia's forty-fifth birthday. They had been best friends for forty-five years. So many shared moments, different countries, men, jobs, and why not say so: fights. Yet they had remained friends through thick and thin and today they would be celebrating together, even if it had to be through a virtual party. After a very disorganized start, Mia managed to "connect" herself to some computer thing Livia had organized online. All of a sudden music filled the garden, and even though I was not exactly in earshot, I could hear it, for it was nice and loud.

All sorts of different faces popped up on Mia's computer screen and she recognized practically all of them. They were Livia's favorite people connecting from their computers from the four corners of the world: dancing and carrying on, each in their own private place. Some in gardens like Mia, others in their little flats. Regardless of the fact that they were unable to hug or kiss one another, as would have been the norm, they were all having a blast.

This was the Year of the COVID pandemic. The year in which the world came to a standstill, but not the year in which love and friendship had been defeated. No: love and friendship were stronger than ever, for they know no barrier. For two straight hours, the music boomed across the garden and Mia danced alone, like a lunatic, but as happy as a lark.

These were strange times, indeed. But she was happy.

After blowing kissing to Livia and her friends on the computer screen, Mia went to rest in her favorite spot in the garden: the hammock that overlooked the woods, whilst listening to the birds and taking in the cerulean sky that seemed to smile at her from up above. She spotted a red paraglider in the sky and as she watched him or her slowly move above her head, she took a deep breath and inhaled the freshness of the recently mowed grass and molding leaves, and slowly dozed off, thinking, as she often did, of the past.

Everything was so different now, and so was Mia. A sea of change had taken over her life, Dad's and Marco's.

And yet her memories were intact. But now the pleasant and happy ones were central stage.

A SEA OF CHANGE

I guess there are a ton of stories that I could keep recounting all sorts of adventures. Some full of laughter, others plagued by tears and drama. Like life itself. There were years that went by as quickly as seconds, and others that dragged on for ever. Some events accompany us till the end, while others, in time, fade away.

But life definitely works in mysterious ways. While on holiday at a Swiss ski resort, dancing her ass off in a club one December night, Mia lost her balance (one more time) and crashed into a champagne-filled table.

"Shit!" she managed to blurt out, *'This is a déjà-vu for the millionth time!'* she thought. As she struggled to get back onto her feet, and was apologizing right and left, someone had gotten a hold of her arm and was helping her up. She immediately recognized the voice that belonged to the hand that held her: *'Shit! This was a déjà-vu, alright.'*

"Hey, new girl, I've missed you."

A handsome, freckle-face was staring right into her eyes. But it was the adult version of the kid from way back when she was still a kid in boarding school.

"*Putain!* What the fuck are you doing here, François?"

It wouldn't be long before these two high-school friends would marry; hardly a year after this fortuitous incident. At their wedding, Marco made a moving speech, which involved monsters, witches, and fairies. Shortly thereafter my brothers were born and Marco, soon thereafter, turned into a man himself. Even if life is in constant motion and things are never the same, some, thankfully, do remain intact. And I can safely say that to this day, The Witches still go crazy when they get together. Isabella loves a woman and hopes to marry her very soon. Charlotte had all sorts of nasty things befall her, but in the end was able to overcome all the adversity and is now the mother of a beautiful girl. Lena continues to grumble but has not given up her penchant for order and cleanliness.

Believe it or not, Livia finally decided to take a vacation the summer of 2010. She needed a break from her lonely hills and opted for Ibiza. Life plays strange tricks and sometimes people are just destined for each other: a month later she was married to Jonas! Ha!

Many lovelier witches and fairies have surrounded my family throughout the years, and I trust they will all remain friends for much, much longer.

MOTHER AND DAUGHTER

It is not easy to describe the unique bond that exists between a mother and a daughter. It is as if a woman were to bump into her long-awaited twin or bosom friend.

From the moment of my birth, when Mia received me into her arms, she realized instinctively that she would never, as long as she lived, be alone again. It was magic, pure and simple. I will never have children, I know, but there is one thing that I can say with certainty, and it is that looking at Mia from above, I am convinced that there is nothing comparable in the entire world to giving birth. No matter how many times: each and every child is a gift of nature and there is nothing like it.

When the disease slowly took over my body, I could not talk or explain what was going on. All I could do was try to cry as little as possible so as not to hurt Mia. But in no time, the pain took over, and the only way I had of expressing it was to shout and shout, desperately looking into Mia's eyes, seeking her love, her comfort, her succor. And it was through this shared pain and anguish that we became more than just mother and child.

We became soulmates. For good. And we continue till this day to be attached to one another as if the umbilical cord had never been severed. It just so happened that one day I was forced to leave Mia behind, in the land of the living. There was no other option. On that day, I floated away as if on a cloud, full of light, comfort, and relief. On that day, the morning's first light caressed Mia's face. She shut her eyes for a split second, but long enough to realize that I was gone. That we'd never be able to communicate like the rest of mortals do.

There would be no more kisses or hugs or words.

Never again.

However, it had been a real experience in both our lives. Even if short-lived, long enough for our love to transcend all human boundaries, physical and mental. And its impact is everlasting. She was lucky, and so was I, and we will be forever grateful for having met and loved each other the way we did and do.

One morning, Mia got out of bed and finally decided to live, trusting that I was not lost. She had come to the realization that there were other forms of living and loving, and she had made up her mind that with me she would choose a way in which we'd be together till the end of time. My time and hers.

ADDENDUM

FOUND IN THE KITCHEN

Strangozzi alla Boscaiola del Ristorante Umbria

3 thick slices of smoked *guanciale*
An abundant bouquet of wild asparagus
4-5 eggs
2-3 tablespoons of olive oil
2 handful of *Parmigiano Reggiano*
400g of *strangozzi* or spaghetti
Lots of fresh pepper
Sea salt

Put the water to boil in a large pot with a big pinch of sea salt.

Cut the *guanciale* into 2 cm pieces and fry them in a frying pan (obviously...!).

As soon as some of the grease has dissolved and the *guanciale* is crispy, take it out (save the dissolved grease and keep the pan to the side as you will be reusing it).

Snap the asparagus into 2 cm pieces from its head with your fingers until they bend (instead of breaking) and throw the rest away.

Place the asparagus in the frying pan with a tablespoon of oil – Fry them for 3 minutes then add 1 small cup of water until they are barely covered.

When the water has evaporated and the asparagus pieces are tender, add the *guanciale* and olive oil (there will also be some of the melted grease from the *guanciale* – this is no diet recipe!) Remove the pan from the heat.

In a separate bowl: break the eggs and mix them with a lot of pepper and one handful of *parmigiano* – mix vigorously with a fork.

The water must be boiling by now, throw in your spaghetti and cook *al dente* (2 minutes less than it says on the package).

When cooked, drain them keeping them very wet (some cooking water needs to stay).

Pour them back into the pot and quickly add in the asparagus, *guanciale* and the eggs.

Mix quickly and add the rest of the *parmigiano*.

Serve immediately (ideally into warmed plates).

Enjoy with pepper and *parmigiano* on the table and drink lots of red wine! Preferably *Rosso di Montefalco*.

Meredith's Mozzarella

A bag of rucola
2-3 big mozzarella
High quality anchovies
Tomatoes (only during the summer, otherwise skip altogether)
Olive oil
Pepper

Lay the rucola on a large plate so that it looks like a nice "green carpet".

Only in the summer, when the tomatoes are sweet and ripe – lay thin slices of tomatoes on top of the rucola.

Cut your mozzarella into slices and place them on top of the tomatoes (or directly onto the rucola if you don't have the proper tomatoes).

Add an anchovy rolled on top of each slice of mozzarella.

Drizzle with your most special olive oil and add some crushed pepper.

Serve as an appetizer with chilled *Prosecco* or shots of frozen vodka (Meredith's favorite).

La Panzanella di Bruna:

1/2 loaf of Umbrian unsalted dried bread or unsalted dried country bread
2-3 ripe tomatoes
A handful of capers
A diced nice chunk of pecorino
A bunch of basil
Black olives to taste
Olive oil and red wine vinegar to taste
Very good canned filet tuna (if you are in the mood)

Put the bread in a bowl and rinse it with water until you are able to crumble it with your fingers. Don't worry if the crust crumbles in bigger pieces … it's part of the trick!

If there is water left on the bottom of the bowl, throw it out.

Peel (if you have time it's better... otherwise don't bother) and dice the tomatoes.

Add them together with the capers, pecorino, and basil to the wet crumbled bread.

Mix thoroughly with your hands.

Taste and add oil, vinegar, and salt if necessary.

Serve coldish like you would a banal rice salad with tuna filets on top (if you are in the mood!)

Perfect with antipasti or grilled meat. Great with beer or anything easy.

Stuffed aubergines à la Zaza:

4 *aubergines* cut in half (if they are the plump long big ones) or 6 little round *ones*
1 can (500g) of diced or peeled tomatoes
400g of ground met – beef, pork or veal or best a mix of the three
1 bunch of parsley (chopped)
1 dessert spoon of lemon zest
1-2 chopped onions
1 mozzarella – diced or thinly sliced
A handful of *Parmigiano*
Garlic (if you can take it)
Fresh chili flakes (if you can take it)
Salt, pepper and a broth cube (if you can find one)
Olive oil
Greek yogurt (optional)

Carve the *aubergines.* Keep the inside and chop it up (put aside).

Drop the carved *aubergines* in boiling salted water for 1 for them to become tender but definitely not fully cooked.

Drain them delicately and place them on a pre-oiled oven dish at room temperature.

Pour a little olive oil into a pan and add the chopped onions. Let the onions fry gently until they become transparent and slightly brown. As soon as they are brownish, add the meat with salt and pepper (a squashed broth cube also always adds some "peps").

Mix thoroughly until the meat becomes slightly cooked, then add the chopped *aubergine* and the lemon zest with garlic and chili flakes – let this all sizzle together continuing to mix for another couple of minutes.

Add the tomato can – If you are using peeled tomatoes make sure to cut off and throw away the hard end (where the stem once was).

Let all this cook for another 10 minutes until the mixture has evaporated most of its liquid.

Add the parsley.

Start heating up your oven at 200°C.

Mix and taste to make sure you have enough salt.

Fill up the emptied *aubergines* with this mixture so that they are nice and full. If there is still liquid in your preparation, leave it in the cooking pan and discard.

Drizzle abundantly with *parmigiano* and add the mozzarella over the top of the *aubergines.*

A few more drops of olive oil will not hurt.

Throw in the oven at 180°C for about half an hour – Check your oven from time to time to make sure the cheese is not burning.

Serve with basmati rice and yogurt on the side (yes, it seems weird but it works...) – As this is quite a heavy dish, serve with chilled white wine (*Lungarotti* is one of our favorite *cantinas*).

Dad's *aglio, olio e peperoncino* Marco style:

400g spaghetti
3 garlic cloves
1 fresh or dried red chili pepper
9 tablespoons of olive oil
1 handful of caperberries cut in half without their stems
2 anchovies
1 cup of chopped parsley
8 cherry tomatoes cut in half or quarters, depending on their size
A small bowl of crushed bread *croutons*

Place the water to boil with a big pinch of sea salt and a spoonful of oil.

Heat the rest of your olive oil in a large frying pan – Watch out not to burn it, it should absolutely not smoke.

In the frying pan:

Add your garlic cloves cut into 4 pieces (for the flavor), or chop it in smaller pieces if you can take the bad breath...

Let the garlic fry for 30 seconds moving it in the pan.

Add the chopped red pepper, watch out for the seeds (remove them before if you cannot take spicy).

Add the chopped anchovies and let them melt, once they are melted.

Turn the heat off and add the capers.

Throw your spaghetti in the boiling water.

Remove them 2 minutes before the package instructions and toss them immediately (keeping them very watery) into the frying pan.

Put the heat back on very high and mix the spaghetti in adding the parsley.

If the mixture looks a little dry, don't hesitate to add olive oil.

Serve immediately into warmed plates and sprinkle with your crouton crumbs.

Put the rest of your *croutons* crumbs in a bowl on the table with extra red pepper on the table and serve with slightly cooled *Chianti.*

Livia's *Frittata ai funghi di bosco*

6 eggs
400g of mixed fresh wild mushrooms
½ a lemon's juice
2 spoons of olive oil
¼ cup of white wine
¼ cup of milk
4-5 finely chopped shallots
2 tablespoons of butter
½ cup of chopped parsley
¼ cup of roughly grated *parmigiano*
Black pepper and salt to taste

Rinse your mushrooms thoroughly removing all the earth and cut off the stems.

Drain and drizzle with your lemon juice.

Heat your oven at 180 degrees.

Take a bowl and in it:

Break the eggs;

Add the milk, the *Parmigiano*, the pepper and a big pinch of salt.

Beat with a whip and set aside.

Fry the shallots with olive oil in the frying pan.

Add the chopped-up mushrooms and toss.

When all is simmering add the white wine, salt and pepper.

Let it cook until the white wine has evaporated and add the parsley and 1 tablespoon of butter.

Mix and remove from the heat to cool off.

Wash and dry your frying pan.

Put it back on the heat and melt your second spoon of butter making sure it is spread evenly on the pan.

Throw the content of the bowl together with the mushrooms in your frying pan with the melted butter and cook until you see that the bottom part of your mixture touching the pan is no longer liquid (it will help if you softly lift the sides with a spatula circling the pan while it's cooking).

Place the frying pan on the top part of the oven with the heat coming from the top and wait until you see the *frittata* becoming nice and gold (about 5 minutes).

Take it out whilst watching out for your hands as the handle is boiling hot!

Turn the *frittata* over on a nice big round plate.

This is great for lunch with a big salad or to place on a table for a buffet meal. Homemade white or red wine will do the trick!

LOST IN FRENCH & ITALIAN

In order of appearance

Tourbillon (F), tür-bē-yōⁿ
Whirlwind.

Merde (F), mɛːd
Shit.

Daschsund, daks·hund
Also known as wiener dog or sausage dog, is a short-legged, long-bodied, hound-type dog breed. It may be smooth, wire, or long-haired.

Come va? (I), comay va?
How are you?

Amore ciao (I), a'mo.re chaw
Hello sweetheart

Gruyère (F), ˈgruːjeə(r)
A classified hard, yellow, Swiss cheese named after the town of Gruyères It is sweet yet slightly salty with a flavor that varies widely with age.

Ma chèrie (F), ma shé·ri
My darling.

Bisous (F), bi·zou
Kisses.

Coup de foudre (F), ˌküdəˈfüdr(ə)
Love at first sight.

La Svizzera (I), La ˈzvittsera
The Swiss (girl).

Strana ragazza (I), ˈstrana raˈgatsə
Strange girl.

Pulce (I), ˈpultʃe –
Flea (friendly way of calling someone).

Come stai? (I), ˈkome staï
How are you?

Che paura (I), ke pa·ù·ra
What a fright.

Si, tutto bene(I), ssì tùt·to bè·ne
Yes, all is well.

Bacio (I), ˈbä:tʃọ
Kiss.

Nada, Niente, Nichts, Rien, naa·duh, ˈnjɛnte, nɪçts
Nothing.

Bravo pour ton expo (F), brɑːˈvəʊ poo-r ˈtʌn ɛkspo
Good job on your show.

Ça va? (F), sah vah
Are you OK?

Ti passo Mamma (I), ti pàs·so màm·ma
I pass you to mom (in reference to passing a call onto someone).

Prediletta (I), predi'lɛtta
Favorite.

C'est moi (F), cé moi̩
It's me.

Je t'adore mais j'en peux plus, žœ tuh·daw meɪ zha(n) peu plu
I adore you but I can't take it anymore.

Dommage (F), dɔ.maʒ
What a pity.

Salopette (F), sa·luh·pet
Overalls.

Dio cane (I), 'ʤ:o 'ka:ne
Goddamn it! / holy dog!

Madonna tisica (I), muh·do·nuh 'ʈ.sɪ.ka
Phthisic Madonna.

Sei bellissima e lascerò tutto per te se me lo permetti (I), 'sɛj bel'lissima è laʃʃ'erò tùt·to pér té sé mé ló per·mét·ì
You look so beautiful and I will leave everything for you if you allow me.

Canottiera (I), ca·not·tiè·ra
Undershirt.

Porca Madonna(I), porca muh·do·nuh
Holy God! (you don't want to know the literal meaning...)

Sposa bagnata, sposa fortunata (I), spò·ṣa ba·gnà·ta spò·ṣa for·tu·nà·ta

Very common Italian proverb which literally means "*wet bride, lucky bride*". It is used during weddings which take place in rainy days.

*Spaghetti alla boscaiola e frittata (I), spah-GEH-tee ah l – l ah bo.ska.ˈjɔ.la é frit ˈta.ta

Boscaiola spaghetti and omelette. In Italian, the word '*boscaiola*' means woodsman or woodcutter. Most '*alla boscaiola*' recipes include porcini mushrooms. Porcini are the king of foraged mushrooms.

*Panzanella (I), panzəˈnɛlə

A Tuscan chopped salad of soaked stale bread

*Mozzarella di bufala (I), mɒtsəˈrɛlə di ˈbufala

Buffalo mozzarella; a dairy product traditionally manufactured in Campania, especially in the provinces of Caserta and Salerno.

Prosciutto e melone (I), proh-**shoo**-toh é meˈloːne

Ham and melon.

Porcini (I), paw·**chee**·nee

Porcini mushrooms.

*Ovuli (I), ˈɔvuli

Ova mushroom or Caesar's Amanita.

Apetto (I), aˈpɛt.to

Three-wheeled light commercial vehicle (literally: bee).

Frantoio (I), fran·tojo
Olive press.

Il futuro(I), il fuˈturo
The future.

Pisse dans ton cul, connard (F), pis/ danz ˈtʌn ˈkʌl kɔ.naʁ
Piss in your pants asshole (or jerk or bastard).

Ma superstar (F), masu·pér·star
My superstar.

mon cher (F), mōn ʃɛʁ
My dear.

Puttana Eva (I), put-tà-na 'hey' vuh
Bloody hell (literally: Eve the whore).

Vernissage (F), ver-ni-ˈsäzh
Preview of and art exhibition.

Gnometto (I), ɲɔmaytow
Little man (an affectionate way of calling a child).

Spaghetti aglio, olio e peperoncino (I), spah-GEH-tee ˈaʎʎo ˈɔljo è peperonˈtʃino
Spaghetti with garlic, oil and chilli pepper.

Bialetti (I), bjaˈletti
Moka pot/ Italian coffee machine. It was invented by Italian engineer Alfonso Bialetti in 1933 and quickly became one of the staples of Italian culture. Bialetti

Industries continues to produce the same model under the name "Moka Express".

Avec la queue entre les jambes (F), a·vèk la kyoo ˌɒntrə /le/ ʒãb
In a cowardly or miserable manner (literally: with her tail between her legs).

Anish Kapoor, uh—n ee sh k uh—p oo r
Well known British Indian sculptor.

Je suis enchantée (F), žœ ˈsʊ.ɪs̯ ã.ʃã.tey
Nice to meet you / I am delighted.

Mise-en-scène (F), miːz ɒn ˈsen
Setting / scenery.

Cristo Santo della Madonna (I), KRIY-Ztuw **san**·tow de-la muh·**do**·nuh
Jesus Christ! (literally: Christ of his mother).

Dîner assis-placé (F), ˈdaɪnəʳ asi plase
Formal seated dinner.

Tu m'as compris n'est-ce pas? (F), tyma kɔ̃pʀi nɛspɑ
You've understood me haven't you?

Je suis désolé, mon amour (F), \ʒə sɥi\ dezɔle /mɔ̃/uh-mour
I'm sorry my love.

In bocca al lupo (I), een boh-kah **al** loo-poh
Good luck! (literally: in the mouth of the wolf).

118

In culo alla balena (I), een ˈku.lo ah l—l ah baˈlena
Break a leg! (literally: 'in the whale's ass!)

LE pAsaGe seKret (Le passage secret) (F),
/lə/ˈpæsɪdʒ/ ˈsiːkrət/
The secret passage.

Toupies Beyblade (F), /tu.pi/ˈbeɪˌbleɪd/
Beyblade spinner.

Putain! (F), /py.tɛ̃/
Bloody hell! (literally: whore).

Guanciale (I), /gwanˈtʃaːleɪ/
Cured pork cheeks.

Parmigiano (I), pahr-mee-**jah**-noh
It is a hard, dry cheese made from skimmed or partially skimmed cow's milk otherwise known in English as Parmesan.

Strangozzi (I), straŋˈgɔttsi
An Italian wheat pasta, among the more notable of those produced in the region of Umbria.

Al dente (I), ælˈdɛnteɪ
Describes pasta or rice that is cooked to be firm to the bite.

Aubergines (I), oʊbəˈʒiːn
A vegetable with a smooth, dark purple skin. It is for a strange reason sometimes called an eggplant in English.

Cantina **(I)**, kan'tina
Wine cellar

Croutons **(I)**, 'kru:tɒn
A piece of sautéed bread, often cubed and seasoned.

Frittata **(I)**, frɪ'tɑː.tə
An egg-based Italian dish similar to an omelette or "crustless" quiche or scrambled eggs, enriched with additional ingredients such as meats, cheeses or vegetables.

ABOUT US

Anne Lamunière (Author)

An Italian born in a Swiss body, the stork definitely made a mistake upon dropping me off. Consequently, after growing up in Geneva, I moved to Italy then to New York as fast as I could. Set design being my first passion, I worked in the restaurant business for years to earn my pennies and loved it almost as much as Broadway.

Having now settled back in my home country for the past fifteen years, my career as a specialist in Post War and Contemporary Art has taught me that everything is possible if you climb on the right trains. And, most of all, that anyone can have multiple exciting new beginnings in life.

Contact: anne@lamuniere.ch

Maria Antonietta Bonacci Potsios (Author)

What do fast food, media, finance, and high jewelry have in common? At first glance, not much, but life has surprises in store for those who love challenges! After a Master's Degree in Political Science and a first job at McDonald's, I discovered the world of the media and developed a passion for storytelling. An international career in Marketing and Communication followed in the field of high jewelry and finance with the certainty that one day I'd write a short story with precious illustrations to accompany it!

My motto: dreams come true if you believe in them and if you have precious friends to help you make them happen.

Contact: marian_potsios@hotmail.com

Florence Schlegel Schürch (Illustrator)

As far as I can remember, I have always held a pencil in my hand. This inclination to drawing added to an attraction for fabrics and fashion led me to a career as a fashion designer in Paris. After fourteen years of an eventful life, somewhat tired of the whims of the fashion industry, love, and a baby on the way brought me back to my hometown of Geneva, to my pencils and my favorite weapon, the ballpoint pen, that once back into service, became the tools of my first passion and now main activity: illustration.

Contact: Florence.illustration@gmail.com

Elie Kerrigan Gurevitz (First Editor)

The shadow of a shadow, or the reflection of a mirror or that of many mirrors. For that, to some degree, is a metaphor of what editing and translating is about. The freedom of anonymity it confers is precious and should be exercised with restraint.

I have worked as a journalist and reporter for over thirteen years, which took me to the four corners of the globe, as a PR executive in Washington D.C. for six years, and a translator and editor for the past eleven years. All three jobs were very different in their day-to-day responsibilities, but they all had one common denominator: the word. Its accuracy was always the ultimate aim; it was sacrosanct. "Words matter" is no cliché.

Contact: elkerre@gmail.com

Table of Contents